SAVAGE

IRON ROGUES MC

FIONA DAVENPORT

SAVAGE

As an enforcer for the Iron Rogues MC and manager of their bar, Talon "Savage" Hughs had seen it all. Or so he thought. Then Tamara Hurst walked through the door, and one look was all it took. His instincts roared to life, demanding he protect her... and never let her go.

Tamara didn't expect to fall for anyone—especially not a broody biker with a deadly reputation. But when she stumbled across a dangerous secret, Savage offered her safety without question. And a place in his arms that quickly became home.

1

TAMARA

The final patient of the day gave me a crooked smile as I slipped the blood pressure cuff off his arm.

"All done, Mr. Jenkins." I typed the last of his vitals into his chart. "Your numbers look better than last week."

"Must be all that green stuff the pretty nurse told me to eat," he grumbled, trying to sound annoyed but not quite pulling it off.

I shook my head with a grin. "Spinach isn't the enemy, no matter what you tell yourself. And don't forget to drink more water, not soda."

He waved me off with a shaky hand, already reaching for the can of Mountain Dew in his walker basket. "I'm eighty-two. If soda kills me, it'll just mean I went out happy."

It was hard to argue with his logic, so I kept my thoughts to myself as I helped him out of the mobile clinic's exam room and down the ramp, watching to make sure he made it to the sidewalk safely before heading back inside.

My legs ached from being on my feet all day, and my stomach gave a low growl of protest. Lunch had been a granola bar around noon that I'd eaten standing up between patients. That was pretty typical for a Monday.

"Hey, Tamara. That was the last one, right?" Marcy asked.

I flashed a tired smile at the nurse who worked most of the same shifts as I did. "Yup, I'm just getting ready to wipe everything down and finish charting."

"Great. Thanks, girl. You're the best." She disappeared again before I could say anything else.

I sank into the rolling chair at the computer station and pulled up Mr. Jenkins's chart, fingers moving from habit. The hum of the AC unit mixed with the occasional creak of the van's frame as it shifted on its tires. Normally, I liked the end-of-shift quiet. But something tugged at the back of my mind.

A weird feeling I hadn't been able to shake all weekend.

It started with a patient whose name I couldn't find in the system. Then a follow-up that never got scheduled. Today, it was a file that had been there on Friday and was suddenly gone when I looked for it this morning.

I clicked over to the database again, hoping I'd just been tired and misspelled the name all three times I typed it in. But I still couldn't find anything as I backtracked through the patient list. There was no trace of her visit. No intake notes, no vitals, no discharge summary. It was as though she'd never stepped foot in the clinic, but she definitely had. I'd taken her pulse myself.

My fingers tightened on the mouse. This wasn't just a typo. Someone had erased the record.

And it wasn't the first time a patient's file had mysteriously vanished.

The chair behind me squeaked. I spun around to find the head physician assistant watching me with narrowed eyes.

"You're still here?" Barbara asked.

I nodded, trying to keep my expression neutral. "Just wrapping up my charting."

Her gaze darted toward the computer monitor. "Having a problem?"

"No." I shook my head and wiggled my hands. "My fingers are moving faster than my brain apparently. Just fixing a typo so I can add a couple of notes to Mr. Jenkins's chart."

"Okay."

Barbara was my supervisor, so I should have asked her about the missing files. But she was quick to write people up for the tiniest mistake. And something about the suspicious gleam in her eyes made me wonder if she had a feeling that I had lied.

She disappeared down the narrow hall that separated the exam area from the mobile clinic's admin side. I waited until the sound of her heels faded before turning back to the computer.

I searched for a few other names I could remember. Two more came back blank, and a third had a discharge summary, but it was dated two days before the appointment. That kind of mistake was hard to make since the calendar automatically chose the current date. Someone would've had to manually change it.

My stomach knotted. I clicked over to the shared folder and scrolled until I found a file labeled Transfers—Internal Use Only. I'd never seen it before.

Inside were spreadsheets of patient IDs, medical testing codes, and off-site transfers. Most of the names were replaced by alphanumeric strings.

I copied everything I could onto my flash drive. It was a cheap plastic thing I kept clipped to my badge for backup copies of clinic protocols. My hands were clammy on the keyboard, but I forced them to keep moving, glancing toward the hallway while I waited for the transfer to finish.

When the files finally finished copying, I clipped the flash drive back onto my badge. Then I shut down the screen and logged out like nothing was wrong.

My heart raced like I'd just run a marathon when I stood and grabbed my bag. I tried to look as normal as possible as I headed for the side door, which was closer to the parking lot and my car. But just as I reached for the handle, Barbara's voice rang out behind me.

"Tamara?"

I turned slowly, pasting on a polite smile. "Yeah?"

She approached with that same neutral tone that always made me feel like I was about to be written up. "Any chance you can cover the morning shift tomorrow? Janie called in sick."

Normally, I would've said yes. Extra hours meant more money for nursing school, so I never turned down an extra shift. But every instinct I had screamed at me to get out and stay gone for as long as I could without losing my job.

I tucked a piece of hair behind my ear. "Sorry. I have to head back to my hometown tonight for some family stuff. Otherwise I'd cover, I swear."

Barbara's eyes narrowed a fraction. "I see. Well, safe travels."

"Thanks." I nodded and bolted before she could say anything else.

As I crossed the parking lot, I glanced back just once—just in time to see her standing near the side door, phone pressed to her ear. Her gaze was fixed on me, and the look on her face wasn't friendly.

My hands didn't stop trembling during the ten-minute drive to the apartment I shared with my best friend Lainie. We'd known each other since kindergarten, so it had been an easy decision when she asked me to look for a job up here and move with her. Even before I found out that I wouldn't need to pay rent because her big brother had paid for the full year in advance so she wouldn't have to worry about money while she should be focused on her studies.

I fumbled with the keys twice before I managed to unlock the door. The second I stepped inside, Lainie popped up from the couch, a throw blanket sliding off her lap. "Whoa. What happened?"

I shut the door and threw the lock, then leaned back against the hard surface, trying to breathe. "I think I found something I wasn't supposed to see."

Her expression flipped from curious to worried in a heartbeat. "You look like you're about to pass out. Sit down and talk to me."

I crossed the room and dropped onto the couch beside her. "I think there's something shady going on at the clinic."

Lainie's eyes widened. "Like what?"

"I couldn't find a patient's file this morning. It was there on Friday. Then it was just...gone. So I checked some more. It wasn't even that many because I was worried about getting caught. But two others were missing, and another had a discharge summary that was timestamped two days before their appointment."

She frowned. "Couldn't it be a system glitch, human error, or something like that?"

"That's what I thought. Until I found a hidden folder in the shared drive." I leaned forward, burying my face in my hands for a second before forcing myself to meet her gaze. "The files inside were full of medical testing data and redacted names."

Lainie bit her bottom lip. "There's probably not an innocent explanation if someone's compiling data in a hidden file."

"And Barbara caught me on the computer. She didn't say anything, but I could tell she knew something was off. Then she tried to get me to work tomorrow, so I told her I was leaving town for family stuff tonight." I paused. "When I walked to my car, she was watching me while she was on the phone, and she didn't look happy."

"Okay, that's officially creepy." Lainie shoved the blanket off and stood. "Get changed. Pack a bag. We're going to turn your excuse for not picking up that shift into the truth."

I blinked up at her. "What?"

"You know my big brother is an Iron Rogue, but I don't think you get what that means. They don't play when it comes to protecting people." She stood and tugged me to my feet. "Beck will know what to do. And if he doesn't, one of his club brothers sure as heck will."

"But—"

"No buts," she snapped, eyes flashing. "You're

scared. Do you really think going back to that clinic before you know what's going on is a good idea?"

I swallowed hard. "No."

"Then get your stuff." Her voice softened as she reached down and squeezed my hand. "I've got you, okay? We'll figure this out together."

2

SAVAGE

"Put it on my tab, dammit!"

I glanced over at the bar and sighed when I saw Junior, one of our regulars at The Midnight Rebel, the bar co-owned by my motorcycle club and me.

Rowan, one of my newest bartenders, raised an eyebrow, silently asking what she should do. As the manager, it was my decision. We had a protocol for shit like this, but Junior had been drinking here for at least two decades. I usually didn't have him tossed out on his ass unless he was making too big of a ruckus.

Lately, he'd been a problem more often. Starting around the time I cut him off from having a running tab that didn't require immediate payment at the end of the night. It was a privilege that was granted to very few people. It had been given to him by Cox, the former Iron Rogues president, who was also the father of Fox, the current prez.

A few months ago, Junior stopped settling his account at the end of each week. I tried to talk to him, see if there was a problem he needed help with, but he'd been tight-lipped. He left me with no choice except to cut him off.

"I'll handle it," Hawk muttered.

He was an Iron Rogues enforcer who worked security for the bar on occasion when he wasn't doing club business or on assignment with Iron Shield—the security company owned by our club and Midnight, another patched member.

"Thanks." I leaned back in the chair I'd dragged to the end of one of the booths, taking in the room with a sharp sweep of my eyes.

The Midnight Rebel was more than just a bar. After the clubhouse, it was the beating heart of the Iron Rogues.

It had an old-school feel, almost vintage, but it was also gritty and pulsed with danger and quiet power. It was an upscale twist on a typical MC bar, with plenty of grit but also masculine charm.

Dim pendant lights bathed the space in warm

gold, casting long shadows across dark-stained walnut and mahogany furniture. The bar stretched long and gleamed with polish, lined with perfectly spaced stools. The wall behind it had shelves of top-shelf whiskey that glinted under the low light. No flash, just strength. Tradition. Power.

Everything about the place was built to last, including the solid wood tables and chairs and black leather booths made for serious conversations. The club's skull-and-handlebars insignia was painted boldly across one wall. A claim of ownership and warning all in one, it dared anyone to forget whose territory they were in.

The place whispered danger and loyalty in the same breath. This wasn't some dive bar in the center of town. It was another sanctuary. The clubhouse was exclusive and secretive, by invitation only. Something that was very rarely extended beyond brothers, their families, and prospects. But The Midnight Rebel was a place outside the compound for us to drink, laugh, and relax with outsiders. Although, the customers were most often people who were loyal to the Iron Rogues.

While we were open to the public, it wasn't a place that welcomed strangers easily. Every knot in the wood grain, every flicker of candlelight on steel and leather, said the same thing. You're either one of us...or you're in the wrong damn bar.

Other than Hawk walking Junior out the door, I didn't see anything else that seemed off. So I turned back to the booth and looked down at the papers and computer set in front of me.

Phoenix, the club's treasurer—and a fucking genius with numbers—was going through the bar's books with me since we were nearing the end of the year and had some renovations we planned to start in January. It was mind-numbing shit, but as the manager and co-owner, it was part of the job.

"You doing okay, baby?" Phoenix asked his wife, Lindsay, softly, rubbing a hand over her swollen belly.

She nodded and leaned back in the booth, stretching her legs out to prop them on the bench seat across from them.

His gentle tone made me smirk, thinking about how he'd been adamant that he'd never let a woman get a grip on his balls. He couldn't have been more wrong because the asshole seemed to have lost all his dignity.

After he finished promising her a foot rub, he caught me watching them with amusement.

"What?" he growled.

I shrugged. "Just never thought I'd see you go so soft."

He rolled his eyes. "Only for her. And our kids. Everyone else still gets a bullet."

I snorted at the thought that what he said was true...unless his old lady told him not to.

"You'll see," he muttered before turning back to the numbers.

The front door opened again, letting in a cool breeze. Phoenix glanced up, and a wide smile broke over his face.

At his unusual expression, I shifted around to see who'd entered the bar and—*holy fuck*.

Phoenix's eighteen-year-old sister walked inside, but it was the girl who followed her that had all of my attention.

She looked about Lainie's age, probably around a half a foot shorter than my 6'3", and despite her clear hesitance, she walked gracefully, with an enticing swing in her hips. She had a heart-shaped face, full round lips, and a straight nose with a tiny sparkling stud on the left side, and the most enchanting corn-flower-blue eyes I'd ever seen. Her golden blond corkscrew curls bounced as she walked, hanging to just below her shoulder blades.

She wore dark green scrubs, but they didn't hide

her full, rounded tits and slender, toned body. I instantly knew that she would fit perfectly against mine.

"Bro!" Lainie screeched, running over to throw herself into Phoenix's arms the second he was on his feet.

"Hey, kid," he greeted her, then grunted, "What the fuck, Lainie? You didn't tell me you were coming."

The other girl hung back, her eyes darting around, clearly uneasy in this environment. Considering how demure she appeared, I assumed the sight of all the muscles, leather, and tattoos made her nervous.

"I wanted to surprise you," Lainie chirped, climbing into the booth to hug Lindsay.

When the other girl's eyes flitted to the diamond stud in my ear, she looked a little intrigued. I suddenly wondered how she'd react to the piercing in my—

My train of thought broke off when Phoenix held out his hand to the girl, my gaze snapping to him. "Hey. I'm Lainie's brother, Phoenix."

Before their hands could touch, I jumped to my feet so fast my chair crashed to the floor as I moved to stand between them.

"That's Savage," Phoenix muttered.

"Talon," I told her, keeping my gaze locked with hers.

"Um, Tamara," she returned.

Beautiful.

"We need your help," Lainie said as she climbed back out of the booth.

I didn't give Phoenix a chance to reply.

"Let's go to my office," I suggested, though my tone made it clear that it hadn't been a request. Without waiting for another word, I grabbed Tamara's hand and stalked to the swinging door behind the bar that led to a hallway where the bathrooms and offices were located.

When we entered the hallway, I blinked a few times to adjust my eyes. The lights were brighter so patrons could easily find the restrooms. My office was the first door on the right, and I pulled Tamara into the room with a vibe similar to the bar's front. Then I guided her to one of the wooden chairs in front of my desk. Because of my height, our knees were almost touching. I liked that she didn't shift away.

I heard Lainie rush through the door but didn't take my gaze off Tamara.

"Tell me what's going on," I ordered, careful to keep from sounding too gruff.

She glanced up at Lainie, who'd come to stand beside her, leaning her hip against the desktop. Lainie nodded, then Tamara's gaze swung back to me and she took a deep breath.

It was the wrong fucking time to notice how the movement made her big tits bounce, but my libido—which had mysteriously appeared after who the hell knew how long—didn't give a shit what my brain thought.

Tamara had my full attention when she began to explain, and I realized she really was in danger.

Her voice was low at first, but I didn't miss the tremble in it. "I work at a mobile clinic as a CAN. I started noticing little things at first. A patient's name that disappeared from the system. A follow-up that was never scheduled. A file I entered myself on Friday that was gone this morning. No trace. Like she'd never even been there."

Tamara's hands were clasped in her lap, knuckles white. I couldn't stop staring at them, then at the faint shimmer of fear in her wide blue eyes. It caused a sharp pain in my chest. I hated seeing her looking scared. I wanted her to know she didn't have to worry, that I would never let anything happen to her. And I really wanted to take her in my arms. But all that would have to wait unless I wanted to risk her freaking out and hightailing her sweet ass outta here.

Pride also pricked at me when, even with her anxiety bleeding through, she didn't stop. Her words picked up speed, like she had to get them all out before she lost her nerve.

"I checked a few others. Two more were completely missing. One had the discharge summary dated before the appointment. And then I found a hidden folder. It was labeled 'Transfers—Internal Use Only.'"

My jaw clenched, and my hands curled into fists, suppressing the desire to reach out and touch her. "What was inside it?"

Her throat worked as she swallowed. "Data. Spreadsheets. Patient ID numbers. Medical codes. The names were all scrambled or redacted, but it looked like a list of testing protocols and transfer locations."

I leaned forward, planting my forearms on my knees. "Transfers to where?"

She shook her head. "It didn't say. Just numbers and initials."

Lainie crossed her arms tightly and muttered, "It

sounds shady. Like something straight out of a conspiracy documentary."

Tamara let out a breath and met my eyes again. "I copied everything to a flash drive. It's clipped to my badge. I didn't know who to trust. I just...knew I had to get out. And Lainie said we should come see Phoenix. When she explained why in the car, I figured if anyone would know what to do, it'd be your club."

Your club.

That hit me in a way I didn't expect. She saw us as a shield, a wall between her and whatever the hell she'd stumbled into.

Damn right.

"You did good, baby," I muttered, standing in one fluid motion.

A thunderstorm was rolling in my blood as I stalked to the office door and yanked it open, then stomped into the hall. When I reached the swinging door that opened to the front area of the bar, I practically ripped it off its hinges.

The place was still calm, only humming low since it was early in the evening.

I spotted Hawk by the corner of the bar, arms folded, posture relaxed as he spoke with Maverick, who stood beside him, sipping from a dark tumbler.

As if they felt a change in the air, their eyes were locked on me the second I stepped out.

They both clocked my expression instantly, but Hawk moved first.

"What happened?" he growled as he moved toward me.

I didn't slow down until I was nearly toe-to-toe with them. "Some motherfucker thought it was a good idea to mess with my girl. Now I'm gonna make sure they're breathin' their last breath."

Maverick raised an eyebrow. "Your girl?"

I didn't blink. "Yeah."

Hawk looked confused, but Maverick just smirked.

"You want to explain that?" Hawk grunted.

I gave them a quick summary of the situation. "She seems smart as hell but scared. Thought she got away clean, but some supervisor watched her when she left. On the phone and looking like she wanted her gone."

Maverick's eyes narrowed, his drink forgotten. "Sounds like they're covering something. Testing? Trafficking?"

"Could be," I growled. "I don't know. But I'm gonna find out. And when I do—"

"You're gonna light the place up," Hawk finished

for me, but only because of my reputation. He wouldn't truly get my mindset until he found the one meant for him. Only a brother who'd claimed his woman could understand the stakes.

"Damn right."

"Savage." Maverick's voice was sharp. "You gotta pull back on the reins, brother. We don't charge in without a plan. We need intel. Need to know who's involved. If there's a trail, we follow it."

I knew he was right, but my reaction to Tamara wasn't about logic. It was instinct.

"You go off half-cocked, and you risk shit goin' sideways and making her a bigger target."

My fists ached from how tight I was clenching them, but I forced myself to breathe. He was right. That didn't mean I had to like it.

Maverick stepped closer, his voice quieter now. "Is she what I think she is?"

There was no hesitation. "Yeah."

Hawk blinked, staring at me as though I'd lost my mind, but I ignored him. I didn't have the time or the desire to justify instincts I couldn't control.

Maverick nodded once, crossing his arms over his chest. "Then we have your back. No one touches her. I'll have Fox loop in our contacts. For now, best she stays with us. At the clubhouse. Full protection."

I didn't even need to think about it. "Agreed."

Then he clapped a hand on my shoulder. "Worry about your woman for now. You'll get to burn shit down eventually."

My jaw ticked as I turned and stormed back to the office. Tamara was still sitting in the same chair, but Lainie had taken my place in the other one. Their heads snapped up when I walked in. Tamara must've seen something in my face because her spine straightened.

"You're coming with us."

Her brows lifted, and she pursed her lips, blue eyes perplexed. "To where?"

"The compound. Our clubhouse. You'll be safe there."

Tamara blinked. "I...what? No. I appreciate the offer, but I can go home. I'll avoid the clinic. I'll be fine."

"No, you fucking won't," I growled. "You said it yourself. That bitch was watching you. They probably know you suspect something. That makes you a target."

"I still have to figure out work. If I can't go back to the clinic, I need another job. I don't have to worry about rent, but I can't live off Lainie for everything else."

I opened my mouth, ready to shut that argument down hard, but Lainie jumped in before I could.

"I think it's a good idea," she said quickly, reaching out to take Tamara's hand. "I can stay with you for a few days. And it's temporary. Until the club can figure this stuff out and make it safe for you to come home."

I didn't bother correcting her. It wasn't the right moment to inform Tamara that she would never be leaving.

Tamara looked between us, clearly still uneasy. "I don't know much about motorcycle clubs, okay? All I know is stuff I've seen on TV, what I've read in books, and the rumors that made their way around this town while I was growing up. It's not like you shared much with me, Lainie, which I totally get. But a motorcycle club doesn't exactly scream 'safe haven.'"

Lainie rolled her eyes and gave her a crooked smile. "Yeah, well, the Iron Rogues aren't like other MCs. They don't do drugs or trafficking. You won't find slutty club bunnies hanging around either. The old ladies would castrate the guys if they ever saw one there. Family comes first with my brother's club. And they protect people. Especially those who can't protect themselves."

Tamara opened her mouth, probably to argue again, but I was out of patience.

"You brought it to us," I cut in, voice low and final. "That means it's ours now."

What I didn't add—what I wouldn't say out loud yet—was simple.

And you're mine.

3

TAMARA

"This is it," Lainie murmured as the guy at the gate waved us through.

In all the years I'd known Lainie, I'd never come to the clubhouse with her. I had only ever met her brother a few times, so I wasn't surprised he hadn't recognized me.

My dad hadn't been a fan of my best friend being connected to the Iron Rogues, but he no longer got a say in my life. Not when I was no longer under his roof. Especially when he sold the house and other properties he owned near Old Bridge the second I got a job and moved in with Lainie. He packed up and moved to Florida because, as he put it, "I don't have to worry about you now that you're an adult."

Talon pulled his bike up next to us. He hadn't

said a word when we left the bar. Just glared at the
passenger seat of Lainie's car like it had personally
offended him. I'd caught the look and felt it all the
way to my toes, but I hadn't understood it—not
really. Lainie hadn't been any help, either. She just
muttered something under her breath and rolled her
eyes when she turned the key in the ignition.

I was hyperaware of him stalking behind us as I
trailed Lainie into the clubhouse. I tried to focus on
where I was walking, but it was difficult when all I
wanted to do was turn around and ask him why he
seemed so pissed off.

"You good?" she asked under her breath.

"Yeah," I lied. "I just didn't know what to
expect."

She glanced at me and grinned. "Don't worry.
Nobody here will be dumb enough to mess with you
while Savage glares at them."

"Except he won't be here all the time," I
muttered.

"That's what you think." I didn't get the chance
to ask her what she meant before a man at the bar
called us over. Lainie laced her fingers through mine
and whispered, "That's Fox, the club prez. If you
think he looks scary, just wait until you see him with
his twins. Jett and Violet aren't even two yet and

already have him fully wrapped around their little fingers."

Picturing the big biker at the beck and call of his toddlers eased a lot of my tension. Clearly, she hadn't been exaggerating when she said these were family guys.

"Maverick said you need a place for you and your friend to stay?" he asked, looking at Lainie.

She nodded. "Yeah."

He jerked his chin toward the hallway on the far side of the room from us. "President's quarters are open since I never use 'em. Has its own bathroom so you'll have as much privacy as you want."

Lainie smiled. "Sounds perfect. Thanks, Fox."

A low sound from behind me cut through the room like a blade. The deep growl made me freeze, but Lainie just giggled while Fox shook his head with a sigh.

Talon moved to my side, his shoulders tense and his eyes locked on Fox as though he was seriously considering attacking his club president.

I looked at him, but he didn't say anything. I didn't even think he blinked while he stared at me. Suddenly, I couldn't breathe right...and it wasn't due to fear over my situation. It was all about my reaction to the sexy biker at my side.

He stepped closer, and I noticed again how big he was. Easily nine inches taller than me, his broad shoulders were tight with tension. His hair and beard were both the same thick, sandy brown, and his gray-blue eyes filled with an intensity I didn't understand.

But then his gaze shifted to me, the diamond in his ear catching the light from the recessed bulb above us as he tilted his head, and something in my chest stuttered.

A pretty redhead walked up to Fox and leaned against his side as she beamed a smile at us. "Hey, Lainie."

Fox brushed a kiss against the top of her head. "Will the kids be busy long enough for you to show Lainie and her friend Tamara to our room?"

"Yup, they're playing with Luna, so Molly told me to escape while I could."

Fox's lips curved into a grin that made him so much less intimidating. "Wanna bet Mav'll check on them when he hears she's on her own with three kids?"

"Nah, that's a losing bet if I've ever heard one. He's just as bad with her as you were with me when I was pregnant." She turned to us and asked, "Ready to head up there now?"

"That'd be great, Dahlia." Lainie tugged on my

hand. "After classes all day and the drive, I'm wiped. And I'm sure Tamara is too since she worked for eight hours before we left."

"I'm sure." Dahlia gave her a quick hug, her affection for my best friend clear. "Two hours didn't sound that far away when you left for college, but it's been forever since we've seen you."

Lainie rolled her eyes. "It's only been three months."

"We were all starting to think college swallowed you whole," Dahlia teased.

"Close enough," Lainie joked back, already falling into step beside her as though she'd never left.

I followed them across the big room and down the hall, feeling like the awkward tagalong who was out of place in their easy rhythm. It wasn't anyone's fault, not really. Dahlia had been nothing but nice. But I couldn't help noticing how easily Lainie fit in here. She was as comfortable as I'd ever seen her.

Dahlia stopped in front of a thick wooden door and turned the handle. Then she pushed it open to reveal a small apartment-style suite that was bigger than I expected. Between the en suite bathroom and kitchenette, I could hide out in here the entire time I was here if I wanted. Except then I wouldn't see Talon, which bothered me more than it should've. I didn't even know the guy, but that didn't seem to matter

"If you need anything else, just holler," Dahlia said with a smile.

"Thanks. This is way more than I expected."

"You're family by extension," she replied. "Which means we take care of you."

I didn't know how to respond to that, so I just nodded and rubbed my palms over my thighs. As Dahlia and Lainie chatted about something I couldn't focus on, I felt it again...that low buzz under my skin. I turned my head to glance at the doorway and found Talon standing there with one hand braced against the frame.

His broad chest rose and fell as though he was holding something back. He didn't step inside, just guarded the door. Maybe it should have freaked me out, but I felt safe instead.

Any ideas I had about hiding flew out the window when Dahlia suggested, "You should hit up the kitchen after you drop your bags in here. Sheila has been cooking up a storm since Tank told her you were coming home tonight."

"Her famous mac and cheese?" Lainie rubbed her hands together. "With roasted chicken and glazed carrots?"

"Yup," Dahlia confirmed with a grin. "Sadie also baked a few pies—cherry, apple, and chess."

"Yum." Lainie dropped her bag on the end of the bed, then grabbed mine and did the same. "We better get down there before all the food is gone. Sheila is Tank's old lady. He's been a patch for basically forever, and her food is amazing."

Talon stepped away from the door, giving us room to get through.

"I could eat," I agreed as my best friend led me back downstairs.

Lainie wasn't exaggerating when she said the kitchen was packed. A few men in leather vests leaned against the counters, eating chicken legs over paper towels. I hovered in the doorway behind Lainie and Dahlia before taking a small step forward.

Talon was right behind me. He didn't say anything and didn't brush against me. Heck, he barely even breathed. But I felt him all the same. His presence filled the space between us, and I didn't have to turn around to know his eyes were on me.

They hadn't left me since I'd stepped out of Lainie's car.

A woman old enough to be my mom rushed over to give Lainie a hug, then surprised me by wrapping her arms around me too. "You two look like you haven't eaten all day. Sit and enjoy a plate of some of Lainie's favorites."

"Thank you." I flashed her a grateful smile. "It's been a while since lunch."

"If you want to call a granola bar lunch," Lainie teased.

"That barely counts." The woman tsked and handed me a napkin. "I'm Sheila. You'll find I don't take no for an answer when it comes to food."

As I sat at the end of the long table, Talon leaned against the wall behind me, arms crossed and jaw tight.

Still silent. Still watching. And somehow, I was more than okay with that.

I kept mostly quiet while I ate, letting the chatter swirl around me as I focused on the plate in front of me. The chicken was juicy, the carrots glazed just right, and the mac and cheese was so creamy it practically melted on my tongue.

When I only had a few bites left, I stole a glance over my shoulder at where Talon still leaned, half in shadow. His silence wrapped around me tighter than any blanket could've.

My dad had basically bailed as a parent when my mom passed away, so I didn't trust easily. But something about the sexy biker made me feel safer than I ever had before. It was why I'd taken my time eating...because I found myself wishing I didn't have to go back upstairs with Lainie. That I could stay in his orbit a little longer...and pretend that I hadn't come here because of the situation I'd stumbled across at work.

The meal finished too soon, and by the time we made it back to the room, my body felt heavy with exhaustion. But my mind wouldn't shut up.

Lainie flopped onto the couch with a dramatic sigh, stretching her arms over her head as though she didn't have a care in the world. "Okay, the food coma is setting in. You good to grab the bathroom first?"

I hovered near the edge of the room with my arms crossed, my pulse still a little jumpy. "Uh, yeah. Maybe in a minute."

She blinked at me, then shrugged and started scrolling through her phone, completely unaware of the storm swirling inside me.

I didn't even know what I was waiting for...until a knock came at the door.

I startled slightly, then padded across the room to open the door. Talon was in the hallway, a folded black T-shirt clutched in his hand.

He stepped close enough to hold it out to me, his

eyes heavy-lidded and unreadable. "Brought you this in case you need something to wear to bed."

I clutched the soft material to my chest, barely resisting the urge to sniff it to see if the shirt smelled like him.

"Need the flash drive," he said gruffly.

Hesitantly, I dug into my pocket for the security badge I'd clipped the drive to.

He watched me with those intense gray-blue eyes, and I marveled again at how this stranger could make me feel so safe.

Holding out his hand, he murmured, "Trust me, baby."

I was completely shocked to realize that I did. Somehow, in the small amount of time I'd known him, he'd managed to gain my trust.

When I set the badge in his hand, his fingers curled around it. Then he leaned in and brushed his lips over my forehead in a firm, lingering touch that sent a shiver down my spine.

"You're safe now," he murmured, the words like a vow. "I won't let anything happen to you."

He was gone before I could react, the door clicking softly shut behind him.

I stood there for a long second, shirt pressed to my chest, heart racing like I'd just run five miles.

"You gonna sleep in that or just stand there holding it all night?" Lainie asked with a smirk.

Heat rushed to my face as I turned away. "Shut up."

We both knew I didn't actually mean it. Not when I curled up on the bed twenty minutes later with Talon's shirt hugging my body...and his scent wrapped around me like armor.

4

SAVAGE

Leaving her room was one of the hardest things I'd done in a long time. The only reason I managed it at all was because Tamara was curled up in my shirt, wrapped in my scent, tucked safe inside our walls. If I hadn't seen her with my own eyes, holding that soft cotton to her chest like it was armor, I would've been parked outside her door all damn night.

That girl was mine.

And now that she was under my roof, under my protection, nothing else took priority.

Not the bar. Not club business. Not sleep.

Only Tamara.

My boots echoed against the hallway floor as I

made my way to the office I had in the clubhouse. I did most of my work at Midnight Rebel, but I was also set up so I could work here.

The air felt different. Thicker somehow. I wasn't sure if it was the adrenaline, obsession, or both. Either way, my pulse hadn't settled since she'd walked into that bar and flipped my world upside down with one look.

I dropped onto my chair and turned on the lamp, shadows spilling across the papers strewn on my desk. Numbers, invoices, bar orders...all of it faded from view as I inserted Tamara's flash drive into my laptop and downloaded all the files. Then I grabbed my phone and hit Deviant's number.

"Sav," he answered on the second ring, his voice low and rough like he hadn't slept in a couple of days. In the past, he probably wouldn't have. But the tech genius's old lady kept him from getting lost in the work like he used to.

"I need eyes on that clinic," I said without preamble. "Cross-check their patient lists and transfers. Look for licensing issues. Track where the money's coming from. Find out if they're backed by anyone—government or private. There's a file labeled Transfers—Internal Use Only. Tamara got it downloaded onto a flash drive. Sending it to you now. She thinks patients are disappearing."

He was quiet for a beat. "You think, or she thinks?"

I leaned forward and growled, "She thinks. So I know."

Another pause. Then a low whistle. "Got it. Want traffic cams, too?"

"Pull everything. Traffic cams. Street surveillance. Anything pointing at that mobile clinic. If you find movement at odd hours or missing time stamps. If something so much as breathes near that place, I want to know."

"On it. I'll ping you when I have something."

I hung up and sat back, staring at the monitor but not seeing a damn thing. The door creaked open behind me, but I didn't need to look to know who it was.

Fox slid onto the chair opposite me with a look that said he'd heard more than I'd wanted him to. Maverick followed, closing the door behind him before leaning against the hard surface with his arms crossed.

"Mav filled me in." Fox's voice was calm but low, his version of warning bells. "Said you had that look.

The one you get when you're itching to make someone bleed and burn shit down."

"Sounds about right."

He watched me for a beat, his expression unreadable.

Fox had cause to be concerned. Few people knew what lived beneath the businessman they saw when they looked at me. I rarely lost control. But when I fought, I did it like I was out for blood. No finesse. No rules. Just raw, unhinged violence that left a message. They didn't send me to talk. They sent me when they wanted someone to bleed.

He leaned forward and cocked a brow. "She yours?"

There was no hesitation. "Yeah."

Fox's eyes narrowed just slightly, his mouth twitching with the edge of a grin. "Thought so."

"Figured Mav would've already run his mouth to you," I muttered, my voice bone-dry and laced with sarcasm. "Thought you two shared everything over pillow talk these days."

Maverick rolled his eyes and shot me the bird.

"He did," Fox replied, ignoring my jab. "Wanted to hear it for myself." His lips curled up a little more, and he shook his head. "Warned you. One look, and you're all in. Already picturing baby booties and car seats."

I gave him a flat stare. "You done?"

Mav snorted. "He's just surprised it hit you that fast. Thought you were immune, but it turns out you just hadn't met yours yet."

"Figured I'd need to chip the ice off your soul before you'd ever fall," Fox added. "The kind to go down swinging."

I leaned back in my chair and smirked, slow and dark. "Still got teeth, boys. And plenty of swing in me. Just might be aimed at any motherfucker who is stupid enough to come near her. And if you two don't stop runnin' your mouths, I'll bury both of you under the new concrete slab behind the garage."

That got a chuckle from both of them. Fox stood and clapped his palm on my desk. "We'll let you keep your pride for now. You decide how to handle shit with the bar, but you're off club business until this shit with Tamara is sorted. That's not a request."

I didn't argue. I couldn't when it was the right call.

"She's your priority now," Fox added as he stepped back toward the door. "Get some damn sleep. She'll need you on your game."

When they left, the silence returned, but I

couldn't bring myself to leave the office just yet. The thought of lying in my bed while she was down the hall in a room too damn far from reach made my skin crawl. So I didn't. I crashed in the empty room next to hers, not bothering to change my clothes. I just yanked off my shirt, kept my jeans on, and lay down on the mattress, staring at the ceiling.

I didn't sleep. Couldn't. Not when I didn't have eyes on Tamara.

The second I heard her and Lainie leave their room in the morning, I was up and in the shower, scrubbing away the restless night. Fifteen minutes later, I was in the kitchen.

Tamara sat at one of the long tables, fresh-faced but tired. Her hair was up in a messy bun that made me want to fist it. She didn't see me at first. I took up position against the wall behind her like a shadow that wouldn't leave.

Her T-shirt and jeans clung to her toned body and slender curves. It wasn't meant to be alluring, but she'd make a potato sack look sexy as fuck. A few of the guys looked too long, but I didn't need to say anything. One low growl, and they suddenly remembered how to find the far side of the room. One prospect walked too close, his eyes lingering, but when I grunted and he looked at my face, clocking my thunderous expression, he turned around so fast he damn near tripped over his own boots.

I didn't touch the food. The only thing I wanted to taste was her.

I didn't sit either. Just watched over her.

Eventually, Wrecker called from across the room. "I'll be at the bar to help open tonight."

Wrecker was filling in because Riot, my assistant manager, was off for the night. Which meant I had to be there.

Tamara laughed at something Lainie said, the sound low and sweet. She leaned forward to take another bite of her breakfast, and my hands curled into fists.

The idea of leaving her, even for a shift, made my jaw lock so tight it ached. But I nodded once.

When one o'clock in the morning rolled around, I was still behind the bar at Midnight Rebel. My patience was gone. The register jammed, one of the taps sputtered, and I hadn't stopped checking the clubhouse camera feeds on my phone. I'd kept tabs on Tamara through security footage and brief check-ins with my brothers. She'd spent the day with Lainie. Met the wives. Played with the kids. Seeing her with my friends' babies made me think about putting my kid in her, and I'd had to adjust myself several times.

I was in the back storeroom, cussing out the ancient register and grabbing a case of whiskey to restock the shelf, when my phone buzzed.

Deviant.

"Got something?"

"Clinic's a front," he said, low and clipped. "Flash drive's files were buried behind multiple security layers. Took me a while to untangle it all. The clinic is being funded through a shell corporation. It traces back to a pharma group flagged twice before for unauthorized biotech trials. We're talking illegal testing. Unlicensed, black-market level shit. It's fucking bad."

My blood turned to ice. "Name."

"I'm sending everything I have now. But I'll keep digging."

I hung up, forgot about the whiskey, and stalked toward the front. Wrecker glanced up from where he was serving a Jack and Coke to some college kid who didn't know better than to be here this late.

"You look like you're about to go full scorched earth," he grunted. "This about your girl?"

I gave him a short nod before running a frustrated hand through my hair.

He didn't hesitate. "Go. I have it. I'll pull in someone from the schedule."

"You sure?"

"I'll let Riot know he's gonna be pulling doubles for a few days. You handle your shit."

I didn't stop to thank him. Just grabbed my keys, walked out the door, and headed straight for the one place I wanted to be.

Back to Tamara.

5

TAMARA

I barely saw Talon yesterday, but every time I turned a corner, I found myself hoping he'd be there. He hadn't said much during breakfast, but I could still feel the brush of his lips across my forehead when he left. I missed his broody presence. Even while hanging out with a bunch of the old ladies in the great room, I kept glancing at the door every time someone walked in. Which was often because a lot of people popped in to see Lainie.

I met Ellery, who brought Corinne and Porter with her. They were dropped off by Whiskey, who'd been on his way to the Iron Rogues' tattoo shop. And Elise with her adorable toddler Toby Jr., who had explained her husband was a doctor pulling a shift at the hospital. Molly and Dahlia were also there with their children.

With six little kids running around, the women were too distracted to notice how often I looked for Talon. Except for Lainie, who'd shot me a knowing glance a couple of times but didn't tell anyone.

As I padded into the kitchen the following morning, I immediately searched for him. I found him seated at the far end of the table, a mug in his hand and his attention locked on the doorway the second I stepped through it. His gaze tracked every step I took.

Lainie steered me toward the coffee first. "We should eat before I leave."

I understood that she had to leave early to make it back to campus in time for her first class of the day, but I wasn't happy about it. I didn't want her to feel guilty, though. Not after she had dropped everything to bring me to the Iron Rogues for help.

So I pasted on a smile and quickly agreed, "You're not going to get an argument from me."

"Yeah, it's gonna be hard to go back to eating on campus and from our freezer," she grumbled.

Sheila patted her shoulder. "I guess it's a good thing I packed a cooler full of home-cooked meals for you."

"Did you really?" Lainie bounced on the balls of her feet. "Have I mentioned lately how awesome you are?"

"It never hurts to hear something like that."

Tank came up behind Sheila and wrapped his arms around her waist, brushing a kiss against her cheek. "Just so long as I'm the only one who shows you how fucking great you are in our special way."

I was still in awe of how the Iron Rogues men weren't afraid of showing how much they loved their women, no matter who was around. They completely shattered everything I thought I knew about how bikers treated their old ladies. And I found myself wondering more often than I should if Talon would be the same way with me if we were ever to get together. I mentally snorted at that. As if that would ever happen.

After filling my plate, I took the seat next to Lainie. Talon didn't say a word, but I noticed how he shifted slightly, angling himself to face us more directly.

After we finished eating, Lainie grabbed her travel mug and slung her bag over one shoulder with a dramatic sigh. "I feel weird leaving before it's safe for you to come back. Maybe I should—"

"Nope," I cut in firmly. "It was one thing to skip

Tuesday since you only had one class. But you can't miss all three today. You'd fall too far behind."

She shot me a guilty look anyway. "I know, but I feel like I'm abandoning you."

"You're not," I said quickly, even though the knot in my stomach tightened the closer she got to the door. I wasn't scared exactly...but without my best friend around, the reality of everything I was facing felt a lot heavier.

Lainie pulled me in for a quick hug. "I'll text and call. Constantly. You won't even have time to miss me."

"Promise?" I whispered.

She grinned. "Cross my heart."

Then she was gone, and I stood there a little too long, unsure what to do next. The easy rhythm I'd fallen into beside Lainie vanished the moment she left, and I suddenly felt out of place.

"You're not alone."

The deep voice came from just behind me, but I knew it belonged to Talon.

I turned to look at him, flashing him a small smile.

"I'm not going anywhere."

Relief swept through me so fast, it nearly made my knees buckle. But there was guilt mixed in with the feeling. "You don't have to stay just for me. I'm sure you have other stuff you should be doing."

"Cleared my schedule." His eyes narrowed slightly. "You're mine to protect."

I wasn't sure what to say, but my breath caught in my chest at the possessiveness in his tone.

The kitchen emptied out gradually, voices fading down the hallway until only Talon and I remained. He just stood there, arms crossed, watching me.

Finally, he said, "Come on."

I followed him through a short hallway and out a heavy metal door that led to a small patio. A few chairs sat around a small table overlooking the trees.

The air smelled like pine, and the breeze cut through the lingering tension in my chest.

Talon pulled out one of the chairs for me, then took the one beside it, stretching his legs in front of him and bracing his hands on his thighs.

"We've been digging into what you found." He jumped straight to it without any preamble. "Normally, I wouldn't be able to share much about club business, but since you brought this to us, I can tell you some of it."

"Like what?"

"We traced the file trail to a shell corporation based in Chicago. They've been funneling money into medical programs in smaller towns, mostly mobile clinics and experimental outreach efforts."

My stomach twisted. "And?"

"Best we can tell, they're running illegal biotech trials." His jaw flexed. "Using underserved communities as guinea pigs. Minimal oversight. Shady consent protocols."

I blinked, bile rising in the back of my throat. "The patients I couldn't find...they were test subjects?"

He nodded once. "Looks like it."

My fingers tightened around the armrests. "I knew something was off, but I didn't think it was that bad."

"You don't mess with people's health." He shook his head, eyes fixed on a distant point in the trees. "Not for profit or convenience. And sure as hell not because you think no one will notice."

A long silence stretched between us, broken only by the wind rustling through the leaves. He didn't look at me, but I felt the shift in the air between us.

There was so much fury behind his words—but none of it was aimed at me. His anger cracked something open inside me.

"I lost my mom when I was fifteen," I said softly, my

gaze fixed on the trees too. It made it easier to get the words out. "She'd been having weird symptoms for months, but the doctors at the community clinic kept brushing her off. Said it was just stress. That she needed to rest more. Eat better. They barely ran any tests."

Talon didn't speak, but I felt the tension in him. How he stilled.

"She collapsed in our kitchen one morning," I continued, my throat tightening as I remembered how scared I'd been back then. "By the time we got her to the hospital, it was too late. She had cancer. It was stage 4. If any of the doctors had taken her seriously before it had progressed that far, she might've had a chance."

My voice wobbled, but I didn't cry. I couldn't, or I'd never stop.

Luckily, Talon remained silent. If he showed me even an ounce of sympathy, I would fall apart.

"My high school had a CNA training program. I signed up for it and earned my certification before I graduated." I shrugged and flashed him a sad smile. "I want to be able to help people more, but I can't afford to go to nursing school yet. I've been saving up for it ever since I got my job."

After another beat of silence, he murmured,

"That's why you looked into it. Even when you knew it might put a target on your back."

I nodded, my throat too tight to answer.

His fingertips brushed over mine where they gripped the armrest. The contact was fleeting, barely there, but it sent butterflies swirling in my belly.

I lifted my head to look at him. He must have moved while I was talking because we were closer than I realized, only inches apart.

Something about his quiet, unshakable presence wrapped around me like a promise.

I appreciated the safety he offered. The strength he wore like a second skin.

But more than that, I just wanted him.

For the first time in my life, I was interested in a man. Actually craved his touch.

I had no idea yet what, if anything, I was going to do about it. With the situation I had stumbled across, the timing was awful. But the urge not to let that matter was growing.

6

SAVAGE

The more I learned about Tamara, the more I liked and respected her. And fuck, I wanted her.

I enjoyed seeing her at ease with me, so I was glad she hadn't realized I was two seconds from bending her over the table and filling her deep enough that she wouldn't remember a world before me.

My control was ready to break. Needing a distraction, I offered to give her a tour of the compound.

As we walked outside, I couldn't stop staring at her. She looked like something out of my dreams with the way her blond curls caught the late morning light as we walked the path around the main compound. I didn't give her a full tour. Just enough to help her get her bearings and satisfy her curiosity, while keeping her far the hell away from places she didn't need to know about.

I pointed out the gun range, a building that Iron Shield's private ops team sometimes used for training, and the back gate that led to the trails through the trees.

She didn't ask about the rest of the land that curved into the tree line, where a small building sat tucked behind brush and a natural slope. A spot on our property that was the farthest from any of the businesses, homes, and clubhouse while still being within the compound's security walls. A place we called "The Room," a name as dismissive as its exterior.

From the outside, it looked like a utility shed or maybe an equipment storage unit. But the interior had four rooms—a lounging area of sorts, a cell, an interrogation hold, and a space that had a cache of weapons and tools. Ones that might be needed to aid us in gaining what we wanted. Like answers. Or just the sound of our enemy's screams.

I didn't bring it up. Didn't plan to unless she ever needed to know what kind of things I'd do to keep her safe. And I'd do every single one of them without blinking.

We returned to the clubhouse, and I showed her the gym and a few other places she could freely go before heading to the garage where we worked on our bikes. She paused, watching one of the prospects shine up a custom rebuild like it was a damn Mona Lisa. Her head tilted slightly, and I caught a soft smile.

I loved that she liked this place. I wanted her rooted in it. Pregnant. Tethered. The kind of belonging that came with sex, bonds, and a future.

Since she'd never been to Iron Inkworks, which was only two blocks away from our front gate, I took her there as well. Watching her light up at the amazing work from our artists had me already planning the ink I was gonna talk her into one day. I'd have my name all over her sexy body if she let me.

Back at the compound, I ended the tour at the playground Fox had built after Dahlia had their twins. Tamara's eyes lit up, and her plump lips stretched into a smile. She was fucking gorgeous. But she was everything when she murmured something about hoping her kids had a place like this to play someday.

We wandered into the kitchen to grab some

lunch. While we ate, she asked me a few questions about the club and the town—from our perspective since she'd grown up on the outskirts. I answered them honestly, even if I wasn't exactly verbose.

Afterward, she turned to me with those cornflower-blue eyes and said, "I've taken up enough of your time. You probably need to get some work done."

"Nothin' I'd rather be doing, baby."

Tamara smiled, but shook her head as if she didn't believe my statement. Then she shrugged. "I need to update my résumé anyway. And start applying for other jobs."

I stared at her.

She blinked.

I kept staring.

She gave me a slow, sassy smile. "You get the need for a job, right? Since you have one? Manager of the bar and all that?"

I grunted and dragged a hand over my face. "Yeah, I have a job. But you don't."

She straightened, and her brow dipped. "I just said I need to get one."

"No." I shook my head, already turning to lead her toward my office. "You don't."

She followed without arguing, but I could feel her gaze drilling into my spine the whole walk there.

Once we were settled with me behind the desk and her across from me, I booted up the system and logged into the bar's security logs. I had the feeds open in the corner of the screen, mostly to keep my eyes on things, but also because I needed something to do with my hands so I didn't grab Tamara and remind her exactly whose shirt she slept in last night.

She was curled into the chair, laptop balanced on her thighs, one leg tucked under her, her bottom lip caught between her teeth while she clicked and typed. Every time she made a little noise of frustration, I fought the urge to stalk around the desk and kiss her into submission. Or bend her over the damn chair and remind her she didn't need a job. Not when I had plans to put a ring on her finger and my baby in her belly.

"You always this quiet?" she asked after a while, eyes still on her laptop screen.

I didn't answer. Couldn't. Not when she stretched her back, arching her chest so her perfect tits were all I could see. My control was slipping like sand through my fingers.

She glanced up, and one corner of her lips hiked up. "Let me guess. Brooding is part of the brand?"

My mouth twitched, and I decided to go for honesty. It was about time she started understanding what was happening between us. "Tryin' to talk myself outta bending you over this desk right now. Figured silence was safer."

Tamara's eyes widened, her breath catching.

I didn't take the words back. Just let them sink in.

She was saved from a response when there was a sharp knock on my door.

"Yeah?" I called.

It cracked open a second later, and Racer poked his head in. "Hey. Fox has been trying to get in touch with you."

My gaze dropped to my phone, and I mentally groaned when I saw a missed call and two texts from our prez. Fuck. I'd been so distracted by Tamara that I hadn't been paying attention to anything else.

"Sent me to drag your ass to his office."

Tamara looked up with a curious tilt of her head.

Racer's eyes flicked to her, then back to me. "Club business."

I gave a sharp nod. "Tell him I'll be there after I get Tamara settled back in ou—her room."

Racer smirked. "Just don't take too long. Told me to interrupt no matter what you were doin'. Not gonna risk Prez kicking my ass for not following orders or take a bullet from you because I saw something that turned you into a jealous bastard."

My eyes narrowed, my tone low and laced with warning. "Talkin' about it makes my trigger finger twitch."

His mouth widened into a grin before he disappeared without another word.

I stood and turned toward Tamara. "Come on. Gotta get you back to the room."

She didn't argue, but I saw the hesitation in her eyes as we walked toward the door. Before we stepped out, she paused and looked up at me through her lashes. "I don't really like the idea of being on my own," she admitted quietly.

"You won't be." I guided her down the hallway, my hand skimming low on her back. "I'll be staying in the room too. That way, we both know you're safe and protected."

She double blinked, her steps stuttering slightly. "Oh. Uh, there's a couch, I guess—"

I didn't reply. Just grunted something noncommittal. She wasn't gonna be on that couch. And neither was I.

We reached the room, and I stepped inside with her, grabbing her hand to keep her close when she started to walk away.

"If I'm gone past dinner," I said, my voice lower, harder, "one of the old ladies will come get you. You eat with them. Stick close. Do not wander around alone. You're not wearing a property patch yet, which means some dumb fuck might think you're fair game."

Her mouth parted, but no sound came out.

I stepped even closer, crowding her until her back hit the wall. "And if anyone touches you?" My voice dropped to a deadly rasp. "I'll rip their arms off and shove them so far up their ass, they'll be brushing their own teeth from the inside out."

Her eyes widened, and her tongue slid out to wet her lips.

Tempting. So tempting. But the prez was waiting, and when I gave Tamara more than just a fast touch of our lips, I was gonna need a fuck of a lot longer than a few minutes.

Instead, I leaned in and gave her a quick, firm, possessive kiss. Just enough to leave her stunned.

"Stay put," I growled.

Then I was gone.

Whiskey, Stone, Hawk, Racer, and Midnight were already in Fox's office when I got there, spread out around the conference table with coffee, attitude, and weapons-grade sarcasm.

Stone and Racer were mid-argument.

"If you jackasses would stop using the legal fund like a damn tab—"

Racer cut in, mouth twisted in a grin. "You love the drama, Counselor. Admit it. Gives you a reason to use all those fancy words and threaten people in Latin or some shit."

"Pretty sure Stone just threatened to sue me for existing last week," Deviant added, strolling into the office through the door on the other wall connected to Maverick's office. He lifted his chin at me in greeting, and every head turned my way.

"Look who finally showed up," Hawk drawled. "Thought you might've gotten tangled in your girl's curls and forgot how to walk."

I ignored him and dropped into the seat between Whiskey and Stone.

"You look like you've been chewing glass," Midnight muttered, cracking a beer.

"Maybe he finally got laid," Racer said, kicking his boots up on the table. "Then again, with that scowl, maybe he didn't finish."

"Keep talkin', and I'll shove that bottle up your ass, glass-first," I threatened in a low steady voice that made it very clear I wasn't fucking around.

Stone didn't look up from the notepad in front of

him. "Don't expect me to bail any of you shitheads out if you get arrested for murder."

Whiskey snorted. "Not the police they'd have to worry about. You think any of the old ladies would put up with that shit?"

No one had the chance to answer because Fox walked in with Mav at his side, both of them carrying the kind of leadership presence that said it was time to shut up or eat a bullet. I sat back, arms crossed and jaw locked tight.

Fox sat behind his desk, while Mav slid into one of the available chairs in front of it. They started with some club business. Gave us the rundown—maintenance requests, an update on a new client, and a few external security concerns in the south part of town. Nothing heavy.

It was a good thing Fox had already excused me from that shit because I wasn't really there. My thoughts kept circling back to the woman upstairs wearing my damn shirt. Imagining her alone. Scared. Vulnerable.

A prolonged silence finally caught my attention.

Mav leaned back in his chair, smirking. "I remember this stage. When I first brought Molly here, I hated to let her outta my sight until I knew she was locked down."

Fox snorted and pointed at his VP. "You threatened to shoot anyone who got within ten feet. Even me."

That earned a low chuckle from Whiskey and Stone.

Maverick crossed his arms over his chest and glared at them. "Like you two were any better."

"Point taken," Whiskey acknowledged. Then he shot me a crooked grin. "You're not far off from the rest of us, Savage."

I mentally sighed. Yeah, when all this was over, I was gonna take endless bullshit for all the crap I'd spouted about the guys being pussy-whipped. Before I met Tamara and realized I would have to eat my words.

Fox's gaze was steady on me as he waited for the verbal sparring to end. "Tamara?" he asked.

"She's squared away."

"Good," Fox said, lifting a brow. "Because this shit's getting uglier by the hour."

"Company's called Arcane Testing Solutions," Deviant announced as he opened his laptop. He punched a few keys, then flipped it around so we could see the information on the screen. "Like I said before, it's a front. All fake. Paper trail loops back to a med-tech investor group. Real quiet. And real fucking dirty."

Stone tapped his fingers against the table. "Preliminary look at the corporation's structure is a legal rat's nest. Shell companies stacked like a damn Russian doll. Laundering grant money through third-party labs, all marked as nonprofit research."

"Assholes," Whiskey muttered, his voice like crushed gravel.

"They're running trials without consent," Midnight added. "Low-income patients and minimal documentation, all buried under false paperwork. This isn't just illegal. It's reckless. And fucking inhumane."

"We take it down," I said flatly. "All of it."

"One piece at a time," Fox agreed, nodding.

"They have an off-site storage house," Deviant added. "That's where the equipment and old records are. We should start there. Could have something we can use to punch a hole through the corp's armor."

Midnight nodded and pushed some photos to the center of the table. They were all surveillance shots of a small warehouse. He glanced at me, and I jerked my chin up in a gesture of thanks. He'd obviously sent someone all the way out there to check it out as soon as Deviant had an address.

"Get in, get out, then level the motherfucking place," I stated without inflection.

"Not yet," Stone sighed. "We do it smart. Get what we need. But don't tip 'em off."

"Relax," Hawk muttered. "Not like Savage is gonna do something impulsive. Never met anyone so in control."

"You wanna see Savage lose control?" Fox smirked, cutting a look to Hawk. "Look at his girl wrong. Just once."

Hawk snorted. "Not it."

"Damn straight you're not," I growled.

After several more hours of strategizing, the meeting wrapped with a timeline and split responsibilities. Stone and Fox were coordinating with contacts to prep for a legal strike once we had the evidence. Deviant was pulling security footage for our entry point, and Midnight was working on getting us past their security measures. Hawk, Whiskey, and I would handle the recon and the actual raid, while Racer was in charge of transport since our bikes weren't exactly stealthy. Plus, we didn't know what we'd need to take with us. If they were as paranoid as they seemed, we'd likely have to take boxes of actual paperwork to sift through, along with any digital files.

With the plan in place, the guys filtered out, but Fox called out for me to hang back.

I waited while he opened a side cabinet and pulled something out.

"Had a feeling." He handed me a folded black leather vest. "Sent it home with Tank yesterday. Sheila brought it back this morning."

Ever since the brothers had started dropping like flies—finding and claiming their women at warp speed—Fox had kept a stash of cuts at the clubhouse so we didn't have to wait for an order to arrive. They already had the property patch, so Sheila just added the names.

I unfolded it slowly. PROPERTY OF SAVAGE was stitched into a black-on-black rocker, with *Tamara* embroidered on the front. Simple. Bold. *Fucking permanent.*

"Appreciate it."

Fox's mouth crooked up at one corner. "Wasn't doing it for you. Did it for the trail of dead bodies you'd leave if she wasn't walkin' around wearing your brand."

It was after eleven when I finally opened the door to her room. I kept quiet, ready to find Tamara curled up and asleep, planning to strip down and slide into bed beside her. I wasn't expecting to find her standing at the window in nothing but my shirt, bathed in moonlight, staring out at the trees.

My body went hard. Fast. And every primal instinct I'd buried since the moment we met surfaced. This wasn't just lust. It was the driving need to *claim*.

I stepped inside, locking the door behind me, my gaze never leaving her. The shirt was so big it practically swallowed her whole. But the light haloed her curls, traced the outline of her bare legs, the curve of her hips, and her perky ass.

I was seconds from losing it. From grabbing her, yanking that shirt off, and fucking her against the window so hard she wouldn't walk straight for a week.

She turned at the sound of my boots, her gaze soft but curious, and I realized she didn't even know what she was doing to me.

That made it worse.

Because it meant this wasn't a game. She wasn't trying to tempt me.

She just was. *Mine.*

And at that moment, with the scent of her skin in the air and the memory of her lips still lingering, I stopped pretending I had any self-control left at all.

7

TAMARA

I couldn't sleep. The bed was comfortable, the room was quiet, and the door was locked. But none of that mattered. Not when my thoughts kept spinning.

Every time I closed my eyes, I saw medical charts and redacted files, patients' names I'd never find again. My chest ached like I was holding my breath and forgetting how to let it go.

I finally gave up and slid out of bed. Padding across the room in nothing but Talon's shirt, I wrapped my arms around myself and stared out the window. I didn't know how long I stood there before I heard the door open behind me.

I stared out at the trees as Talon stepped inside

the room, quietly shutting the door behind him. When I turned to look at him, I saw that his shoulders were tight, his jaw set, and his hair looked like he'd run his fingers through it a dozen times.

Then his gaze landed on me and dragged down the length of my body. His eyes turned even more intense. Practically burning.

My knees went weak at his look, and I gripped the window frame to hold myself up.

He didn't say anything at first. Just stood there, fists clenched at his sides as though he was trying to hold himself back.

"I couldn't sleep," I whispered.

His eyes were storm-dark now, heavy with heat and something deeper as he took a step forward. Then another.

"I keep telling myself to go slow," he muttered, as though he was talking to himself more than me. "You've been through too much. You need time. Space."

I swallowed hard. "But?"

His chest rose on a sharp inhale. Then he exhaled through gritted teeth. "Fuck it."

I barely had time to blink before I was in his arms. His mouth crashed down on mine and stole every thought from my head. My lips parted, and his tongue swept inside.

Nothing about his kiss was soft or tentative. It demanded everything.

It didn't take long for me to melt into him. As I clung to his shoulders, Talon angled his head to deepen the kiss. All I could do was hold on while he devoured me.

His hands slid down to my hips and gripped hard, dragging me against his chest like he couldn't stand even an inch of space between us. I gasped, but the sound disappeared into his mouth.

Our tongues tangled, and his teeth nipped at my bottom lip before he lifted his head to stare down at me. "If you need more time, you gotta tell me now, baby."

I was overwhelmed by how fast everything was happening, but I knew what I wanted. So I didn't hesitate to say, "I don't need anything except you."

A groan tore from his throat, and then I was swept off my feet. He carried me across the room as though I weighed nothing. One of his hands fisted the back of my shirt—the one he'd given me the first night—as though he was afraid I'd disappear if he let go.

He laid me on the mattress like I was something

precious, even as his eyes burned with sensual intent. Then he trailed his mouth down my throat, and my heart pounded with need.

When he pulled away, I let out a small whimper.

"Don't worry, baby. I'm not going anywhere. Been holding back since the second you walked into that bar. Not gonna waste my chance now that I have you under me."

He stripped his leather vest and shirt off in one rough motion, and my gaze swept down his broad chest to take in the black ink on his right shoulder, side, and hip. When I met his gaze again, his eyes were full of heat. "I'm glad you finally stopped."

His hands tugged at the bottom of the shirt. The one I'd slept in since I got to the compound.

I arched my back off the mattress to make it easier for him to rip the material over my head. After he tossed it on the floor, his gaze focused on my chest. My breasts ached, nipples pebbling under his stare.

"Fuck, baby. Your tits are so damn perfect."

He lowered his head, and his beard scraped against my skin as his lips wrapped around one of the stiffened peaks. My fingers delved into his thick hair, and I shivered against him when he sucked my nipple into the back of his mouth.

"Oh, wow," I breathed.

His gaze locked with mine. "Like that, baby?"

"Uh-huh."

"Good 'cause there's a fuck of a lot more where that came from."

He kissed his way across my chest to give the other side the same treatment, and I felt the tug of his lips all the way to my core.

"This too?" he rasped, nibbling down my rib cage.

"Yes," I panted, gripping the sheet in my fists.

He scooted down, leaving a trail of heated kisses in his wake. I shivered when he circled his tongue around my belly button.

"Can't wait to taste you."

His breath was a puff of hot air against my panties, the only piece of clothing I had on. But not for long.

He ripped them from my body. Then he wedged his broad shoulders between my thighs and lowered his head to lick between my pussy lips before his tongue circled my clit. I'd never felt anything like it before. His touch was warm, wet, and firm. I wanted more...for it to never end.

Bucking my hips up, I rode Talon's face while he ate me like a starving man. He switched up his licks

—long and slow, short and fast. Sometimes hard. Other times soft.

There was no pattern, so I never knew what he was going to give me next except for a lot of pleasure. It built in my body until I was on the edge. Then he pinched my clit, and I flew apart.

He licked me through my orgasm, not letting up until he'd made me scream his name. "Talon, yes! Oh yes!"

My release left me feeling boneless as I practically melted into the mattress, but he wasn't finished.

"Gimme another, baby," he growled against my pussy.

This time, he inched a finger inside as my pleasure ratcheted higher. It was almost more than I could bear as he used his tongue, lips, teeth, and hand to bring me to the brink of another orgasm. Fireworks went off behind my eyelids as my release crashed over me, even stronger this time.

"That's my good girl." My inner walls fluttered at his praise, and he chuckled. "You like me calling you that."

I pressed an elbow into the mattress and flashed him a dazed smile. "You could put it that way."

"I'll be sure to use it more often."

Getting to his knees, he removed his jeans and

boxer briefs and kicked them off the bed, his hard dick springing free. The piercing on the underside of his shaft captured my attention. "Whoa."

His lips curved into a smirk as he wrapped his hand around his thick shaft. "Don't worry, baby. After those two orgasms, you're ready to take me. And I promise, you'll like my piercing a fuck of a lot when it's inside you."

Suddenly nervous, I licked my lips. "Um, I should probably tell you..."

"What, baby?" he asked, settling between my legs with his dick cradled in the apex of my thighs.

"I'm a virgin."

His biceps flexed as he stared down at me, his eyes heating even more. "I'm the first man who's gonna get inside your sweet-as-fuck pussy?"

I nodded shyly. "Yeah."

He leaned down and captured my mouth in a deep kiss that left me breathless. "Such a good girl, saving that cherry for me."

Hearing him call me that when the tip of his dick was pressed against my core, and the cold metal of his piercing teased my clit, was even better. But the pleasure was quickly replaced by pain when he pulled his hips back and drove balls deep inside me with one powerful thrust.

Digging my nails into his shoulders, I chanted, "Crap. Crap. Crap."

"Sorry, baby." He kissed away the tears streaming down my cheeks. "Figured it'd be better to get the hard part over before you had the chance to tense up and make it worse."

"I guess you'd know best," I mumbled before pressing my face against his chest.

"Never took someone's virginity." His palm slid between us to cup my breast, his thumb flicking over my nipple. "And it's been longer than I can remember since I've so much as looked at a woman, let alone fucked anyone."

I loved knowing that I was Talon's first virgin and the only woman who'd caught his interest in so long. About as much as the pulse of pleasure I felt when I wiggled my hips.

"Better now?"

I circled my hips again. "Yeah."

"Thank fuck," he groaned.

He grasped my waist hard enough that I was probably going to have bruises in the morning, but it only turned me on more to know that I'd shredded his control so much. He held me in place while he pulled back, his shaft dragging against my inner walls.

When only the tip was still notched inside me, he slammed back in again. "Fuck! You feel so damn good, baby."

His pace was slow and steady at first, but as my pleasure started to ramp up, he began to move faster and harder. Any hint of my earlier pain was gone, and I met him thrust for thrust. His piercing hit something inside me that was driving me wild. "Yes! More. Please, Talon!"

"Your pussy is so hungry for my cock. Come for me again, baby," he demanded. "Be a good girl and give me another one before I fill your pussy with so much come it'll be dripping down your thighs for days."

His dirty words were enough to push me over the edge. "So close. I think I'm going to—"

My sentence was broken off by my strangled cry as a tidal wave of pleasure crested over my body.

"Fucking hell, baby! Your pussy is milking my cock so good." His hips pumped a few more times before he anchored his dick all the way inside me and groaned with his release.

We lay there for a while, his body wrapped around mine as our breaths came out in ragged pants. My heart beat erratically, but so did his. With my ear pressed against his broad chest, I heard the rapid thumps. Between listening to that rhythm and experiencing three mind-blowing orgasms, I couldn't keep my eyes open.

The last thing I heard as I drifted off to sleep was, "There's no going back now, Tamara. You're mine."

8

SAVAGE

The sun barely crested the trees, but I was already wide awake. Flat on my back, one arm tucked behind my head, the other wrapped around the softest damn thing I'd ever held.

Tamara. Naked, warm, and curled into me as though she'd always belonged there.

Because she had. It seemed like my body had been created with just the right spot to fit her against me like the final piece of a puzzle.

One of her thighs was slung over mine, her bare chest pressed against my ribs, her breath soft where it hit my skin. My hand rested on the curve of her hip, and fingers were splayed possessively. My cut hung on the chair across the room, but she was the only brand that mattered.

I was as much hers as she was mine.

My eyes roamed, slow and greedy, soaking in every inch of her I could see in the glow of early light cutting through the window shades. Her silky curls were a riot across my chest, and her skin bore faint traces of where I'd held her and where my mouth had marked her last night.

A raw, vicious heat surged through me again, causing my dick to swell at the memories.

I hadn't made love to her.

I'd taken her.

Not rough, but not gentle either.

And now that I'd had her, I was ruined. She was what mattered most, and I needed her just to survive. Without her, this life would mean nothing.

Her lashes fluttered as she shifted, just enough to drag her bare center against my hard length. I groaned, the sound low and muffled when I buried my face in her hair.

"Morning," she whispered, her voice still hazy with sleep.

"Hey, baby." My voice came out rougher than I meant it to.

She tipped her head back, cheeks pink already. "So, uh...is it normal to feel, um, sore and sort of... um...stretched?"

I chuckled, and she slapped my chest with a mock glare. "It's not funny!"

"I think you complaining about the size of my dick is the best compliment I've ever gotten," I drawled.

Her face turned redder. "I didn't say that!"

"You implied it, baby." I leaned in and kissed her temple, slow and tender, just because I could. Because I wanted to.

Her mouth softened into a shy smile, and something tight in my chest cracked. I wasn't sure when the hell I'd gotten so mushy, but when it came to Tamara, I didn't care. The guys could give me all the shit they wanted. When it came to my girl, I had no problem being whatever she needed. Even if it made me look like a whipped pussy.

Around people outside the club, there was a protocol. We treated our old ladies with respect but made sure to show that they knew their place. It contributed to our reputation of being ruthless and lethal as fuck. Otherwise, we'd be constantly challenged for our territory.

But within the family, Tamara could ask for anything, and if it was within my power, I'd give it to her.

I kissed her trembling lips, and things started

heating up again. She shifted, and the friction between us woke up every need I'd shoved down while we slept. But when her hands started roaming toward my shaft, I came to my senses and pulled back with a curse.

She looked up, surprised and nibbling on her lip with worry. "Did I do something wrong?"

Seeing her hesitation killed me. "Absolutely not. Any other time, you can touch me as much as you want. But today?" I shook my head and cupped her tender pussy. "Gonna hurt worse if I don't give you time to heal. And I have plans for this hot little body."

"Oh," she breathed, clearly torn between disappointment and relief.

I kissed her forehead, nose, then lips. "Definitely not gettin' out of more, baby. I'm just makin' sure the next round won't leave you limping for a damn week. Need you in prime condition for what I have planned." I grinned and winked at her. "Gotta make sure you never forget who you belong to."

That earned me a huff and a swat to the chest. "Caveman."

"Bet your sweet ass," I muttered, rolling out of bed.

I ran her a bath—hot and full of whatever

fancy crap Dahlia had left in the room—and warned her not to so much as touch the doorknob until I got back. She rolled her eyes but didn't argue.

I hauled ass to my room, packed a bag, and brought it straight back. This was our room now. At least until we found, or built, our own house.

In the meantime, she wasn't leaving it without me by her side. Not unless I'd vetted the people she was around and trusted them not to breathe wrong in her direction.

Then I headed to the kitchen, grabbed two breakfast sandwiches, coffee, and fruit, and brought it back up.

She was in another one of my shirts, and my lips curved into a satisfied grin when I realized she'd deliberately dug through my duffel for something of mine to wear. It hung halfway down her thighs and made her look even more edible. She was perched at the little table in the living room area when I walked in.

"You gonna feed me or eat me for breakfast?" she teased.

I grunted, scowling because now that was all I could think about. But a slight rumble from her stomach brought me back to the present.

I placed the sandwiches on the table, then slid a coffee toward her. "Eat first. Then we talk."

"Talk about what?" she asked as she unwrapped the sandwich from the paper towel to take a bite.

I took the seat across from her, giving her a hard look. "Tonight's raid."

Her spine straightened, and her hands froze halfway to her mouth. "You're going after them?"

"A storage site," I clarified. "Just the first step."

"Who all is going?"

"Hawk, Whiskey, Midnight, and me. Deviant's running comms, and Racer will drive."

"I should come." She stated it matter-of-factly, then took a calm bite of her breakfast, as if she hadn't just suggested I let her walk into the lion's den.

My head snapped up, and my voice was cold as ice. "No. Hell fucking no."

Tamara frowned as she chewed and swallowed. "But I'll know what we're looking for—"

"Doesn't matter," I interrupted, my voice sharp as I slashed a hand through the air. "Not takin' you into a situation that could go sideways."

"You're being ridiculous."

"Protective," I corrected.

"You mean caveman," she volleyed back.

I leaned forward, eyes locked on hers, completely

unapologetic. "I'll stop being a caveman when I can breathe again without worrying about someone hurting you."

That shut her up.

As she sat there staring at me, her expression softened. Then the moment passed, and she sighed. "You're still gonna be a caveman when I'm safe. Aren't you?"

I smirked. "Probably. You'll get used to it."

She rolled her eyes, but the smile tugging at her mouth gave her away.

Later that night, the ride out was quiet. Just engines, wind, and adrenaline humming under our skin. Two hours of tension. Of planning. Imagining every way this could go wrong.

The air was cold and sharp, slicing across our faces as we carved down backroads and dark stretches of rural highway. No one spoke. No one needed to. We were locked in, mentally running through the angles, ready to go feral if it came to that. The only sounds were the rumble of our Harleys and the occasional crunch of gravel under our tires when we peeled off the pavement for a breather.

Despite my focus on the situation ahead, I couldn't stop thinking about Tamara. Every second I was away from her was a test of restraint I didn't have. I couldn't stop thinking about her soft skin under my hands, the sweet taste of her mouth, or the way her body gripped mine like she'd been made just for me.

I needed to get back to her. To touch her. Taste her. Bury myself so deep she never forgot who she belonged to. My chest ached with it...like the ghost of her body was still wrapped around mine.

9

SAVAGE

By the time we reached our destination, I managed to steer all of my concentration on the job. We parked our bikes four blocks up, behind an abandoned warehouse with rusted scaffolding and shattered windows. The place reeked of mold and piss, but it offered cover, and that was all we needed. Our boots hit the pavement with quiet purpose, the weight of our cuts and weapons like a second skin.

Racer was already in position, the van idling in a narrow alley behind the storage facility. The windows were blacked out, and the plates were pulled. The back doors were cracked just enough to start loading fast if it came to that.

Deviant was patched into the facility's outdated

camera system, feeding us real-time visuals. His voice came through our comms. "You're clear. No movement on cameras. Motion sensors are cheap models, blind to anything under six feet. Move now. Stay fucking low."

The building sat low and square—plain concrete and no signage. Just one flickering exterior light above the back door. It cast a dull yellow tint across everything, making it look as sick as the bastards who owned the place.

The back door had an electronic keypad—more secure than most storage joints in a town like this. Someone wanted to keep people out. That was reason enough to burn the place down.

I checked my phone for the code Midnight had texted, then keyed it in. "Showtime," I muttered.

The door gave way with a soft click, but it seemed louder than a gunshot in the silence. My instincts were on high alert, and my hand itched to reach for my gun as I pushed the door open.

Inside, the air was stale and...just fucking wrong. Almost sterile, like someone tried too hard to erase what'd been done here. The fluorescent lights overhead buzzed to life one by one, flickering like we were on the set of a horror movie. Rows of steel shelving stretched into the distance, each one stacked

with neatly labeled boxes, plastic bins, and rein-
forced storage crates.

My lips curled in disgust. It smelled like bleach
and paper. Secrets and rot.

We split up automatically, each of us clear on
our mission. Midnight and I veered toward the far
end where the computers were. It was the only room
with an actual desk and climate control. Whiskey
and Hawk peeled off to work the physical files.

Every few seconds, Racer would appear to grab
whatever he could carry from the boxes they were
stacking to be taken from the warehouse. Patient
records. Sample kits sealed in biohazard bags. Ledger
books full of handwritten entries with dates, dosages,
and initials. Bribes.

I dropped to one knee in front of the main
desktop unit and powered it up. The computer
blinked awake, slow as molasses, so my patience was
wearing thin by the time I tapped in the code
Deviant had hacked to get me into their system. The
files weren't encrypted. Sloppy. Too confident. But
since that worked in my favor, I felt an evil satisfaction at showing them just how vulnerable they really
were. I plugged in a portable drive and started
ripping everything—internal emails, spreadsheets

tracking "compliance failures," payrolls with suspicious gaps, and records of "postmortem processing."

Midnight set up a surveillance tap while we were at it, just in case they got cocky and came back.

One email caught my eye. It was sent from a burner account to the head of operations. "Mother made contact. Subjects to be relocated within seventy-two hours. No loose ends."

I took a screenshot of it, then pulled up the surveillance log and looped the camera feeds before installing a remote tap. If they came back, we'd see it.

Eventually, Hawk came in and started digging through a filing cabinet behind me. After a few minutes, he cursed, his voice tight with rage. "These are consent forms, but they're forged." He handed a stack to Whiskey, who'd stomped in a few seconds before, and he started shuffling through them. "Look, signatures are damn near identical across multiple files."

Whiskey let out a sharp breath. "What the actual fuck? There's an invoice here marked 'recovery payout.' Looks like a fucking death benefit."

Fury filtered into my blood, burning me from the inside. Who would have received that payout if they'd managed to silence Tamara? I had to shake the thought before defying orders and destroying the place in a rage.

Racer returned, sweat slicking his brow despite the chill. "We're gonna need another van at this rate. They have an entire aisle of sealed evidence kits."

"Then load fast," I snapped, not looking away from the monitor. "Don't have time to pick and choose anymore. We take it all."

Ten minutes passed. Then twenty. The silence thicker with each tick of the clock, knowing we were pushing our luck the longer we were there.

Deviant's voice cracked in again. "Motion sensor tripped on the east side. You've got five minutes, tops."

"Wrap it up," I ordered. "Now."

After yanking the drive free, I double-checked the tap. The green light was blinking, indicating that it was still live.

I slipped the evidence into my inside vest pocket and stood, glancing back once at the space with a dark scowl. Sometime soon, I was gonna blow this motherfucking building apart. Preferably with some of these assholes inside.

We loaded the last of it in silence.

Outside, the November air was colder, with a bite to it. But I didn't really feel it, I was still warm from the adrenaline. Racer had the doors open, and the van sagged under the weight of what we'd taken.

Finally finished, he slammed the doors to the back of the vehicle shut. We stood there for a beat, feeling the heavy weight of what all this proved.

Then Hawk said what we were all thinking. "This isn't just paper and files. This is ammunition."

"Good," I muttered. "Because I'm done watching. I'm ready to light the whole damn place up."

During the ride back to Old Bridge, I was coming undone thinking about Tamara. How she'd clung to me, wrapped tight around my cock, breathy and begging. Her skin, her scent, the way she looked after I filled her... it was burned into my skull, and I needed her like oxygen.

The vest in the back of my closet was like a beacon showing me the way home. But I didn't want all this shit hanging over us when I gave her the cut and my ring. The one I'd ordered the first night I slept in the room beside her and was just waiting to be delivered since it was custom.

Until then, I'd focus on giving her something else. A part of me. Something amazing that we created together. And one more tie that would bind her to me forever.

My speed increased as if I were being chased.

Driven by the need to be with my woman and knock her the fuck up.

When we arrived, I handed everything off to Fox and Stone without a word, then headed straight for Tamara. They'd take care of the media drop and coordinate the legal strike. Rip the corporation to shreds in such a public forum that they'd be black-balled from the industry. As well as tied up in arrests and lawsuits until the devil came for what was left of their souls.

But it wasn't enough for me.

Because all I could think about was the men who'd built this. Who'd hurt people. Who'd scared my woman and put her in danger.

They were going to pay. In blood.

A few minutes later, I slipped into our room, quiet as the space between heartbeats. She was in bed, soft and warm, her curls splayed across my pillow.

I stripped down and climbed in beside her. She was half asleep, body pliant and warm when I pulled her into me.

She stirred, murmured my name, and turned to face me.

When my hand skimmed under the shirt she

wore—mine—and found bare skin, she gasped softly, eyes fluttering open.

Her voice was a whisper, but it roared in my ears, filling me with desperate hunger. "Talon."

I kissed her like a dying man. As though she was oxygen and water. She was the last thing keeping me from tearing the world apart. The only thing keeping me sane.

There was no slow buildup. No teasing. Just a collision of mouths and a melding of our mutual desperation.

My hands were everywhere—removing her shirt, gliding over her slender curves, cupping her incredible tits. Her tight little nipples scraped my palms, and my rock-hard cock turned to pure steel.

She moaned, arching into me, her leg sliding up and over my hip.

"Tell me you're okay," I growled, voice scraping the edge of control.

"I'm better than okay," she whispered, nails digging into my shoulders. "I've never felt safer."

That broke the last thread.

I rolled her under me, settling between her thighs like it was where I was meant to be. Her skin was hot, her eyes glassy with sleep and want. She reached for me, and I caught both her wrists in one hand, pinning them above her head against the pillow.

"You belong here, baby," I rasped. "In this bed. Under me. Full of me."

Her thighs widened, hips tilting, silently begging me in the dark.

I thrust into her in one long stroke, burying myself to the hilt with a guttural moan. Her head tipped back, eyes closed and her lips parting in a cry that went straight to my dick.

Tight, warm, already dripping for me. *So damn perfect.*

I ground my hips down, locking her in place while I fucked her slow and deep, each roll of my hips a promise. My name spilled from her lips between ragged breaths, but it wasn't enough. I wanted her to scream it. To have it echoing off the walls, torn from her soul. Telling the world that she was mine.

She tried to move, to take a little control, but I tightened my grip on her wrists and held her down with my hips.

"No," I growled. "I'm not letting you pretend this is anything but what it is."

She blinked up at me, breathless. "And what is that?"

"A fucking claiming."

I shifted one hand to her throat—not squeezing, just holding, grounding her while I fucked deeper. Her pupils blew wide, nearly eclipsing the soft blue irises. Her legs trembled as her climax neared.

"This isn't just sex, Tamara," I rasped. "This is me inside you, putting a future in you, tying you to me in every fucking way."

Her breath hitched, but a spark in her eyes and the pretty flush on her cheeks told me she liked the idea.

"You want that? Does my good girl want me to put a baby in her belly?" I nearly blew just from saying it out loud while her walls clenched around me.

"Yes! Talon!"

"That's right, baby." I thrust again, harder this time, and her back bowed off the bed. "Say it. Tell me who's inside you. Who owns you."

"You do," she gasped. "You. Only you."

"Good girl," I praised before I dropped my mouth to hers again, kissing her with everything I wanted to say but couldn't get past my grunting and erratic breathing as I fucked her with a primal instinct. She'd called me a caveman, and at that moment, I couldn't disagree because I was focused on two things—bringing my woman ultimate pleasure and breeding her.

When I felt her tighten around me, just seconds from unraveling, I let go. Coming with a growl against her mouth, holding her so tightly she couldn't forget it even if she tried.

There was a moment of silence as though the world was holding still. Then she threw back her head and screamed my name as she broke apart beneath me.

When the aftershocks faded, I gathered her into my arms, and we drifted to sleep.

I stayed buried deep.

Because I wasn't done.

I'd never be fucking done.

10

TAMARA

Waking up wrapped in Talon's arms was almost as good as the orgasms he gave me. Each time we had sex, it somehow managed to top the last. Last night was no exception.

He'd gotten in late. I'd almost convinced myself he wasn't coming back until morning. But the second the door opened, everything inside me settled. He hadn't said much, just kissed me like he was drowning. Then he sank into me as though I was the only thing keeping him alive.

There had been less dirty talk than usual, but I didn't need words when I had the weight of his hands and the raw heat in his eyes. And the powerful thrusts as he buried himself inside me over and over again. It hadn't been slow or soft, and I could still feel where he'd been this morning.

Now I lay tangled in Talon's arms, the early morning light filtering through the slits in the blinds. His breathing was slow and steady, and he had one heavy arm wrapped around my waist, anchoring me against the comforting rhythm of his chest as it rose and fell.

I slowly twisted in his hold so I could peek at him. His face was softer in sleep, less guarded, with the sharp lines of his jaw relaxed. I couldn't stop staring at him.

Everything with the clinic was still a mess, but here in his arms, I felt safe. Like I wasn't in this alone.

My phone buzzed on the nightstand. I froze for a second, reluctant to move and risk waking Talon. He hadn't stirred yet, and I knew he needed the rest. But not answering could just as easily disturb him, so I reached out carefully and snagged the phone, slipping it out from under the charger and easing away from the warmth of his body. Then I padded to the bathroom and shut the door behind me before swiping to answer.

"Hello?"

"Tamara? I'm so glad you answered."

I didn't immediately recognize the voice because it was out of context. She had been friendly enough at work when we were on the same shift but had never had to call me before. "Marcy?"

"Yeah, I...um...wasn't sure if you'd be able to talk wherever you are."

Her fear was obvious, and my stomach dipped. "What's wrong?"

I sank onto the closed toilet lid, my heart thudding. "Did something happen?"

"I've been trying to convince myself the weird things I noticed were just administrative screwups or maybe incompetence. But then you left, and I couldn't stop thinking about what scared you enough to walk away without saying goodbye. It's been eating me up inside ever since you didn't show up for your shift on Wednesday."

"I'm sorry for scaring you." I closed my eyes. "You weren't wrong to be worried, though. Something *is* going on, and it's bad."

"I figured." Her voice wobbled. "I snooped around a little and asked questions I probably shouldn't have. Then today, I heard something."

"What was it?"

Her voice lowered as she answered, "Barbara

was on her phone and said something about how they have another trial run scheduled in a few days."

I stilled. "Do you know what it's for? Did she say anything else?"

"No. And not that I heard. I was too scared that I'd get caught eavesdropping to stick around. But whatever this is...it's not above board. I can feel it in my bones."

I let out a long, slow breath. "Thanks for telling me."

"I'm scared, but not saying anything felt wrong," she whispered.

I understood the feeling. "You did the right thing. I promise I'll do something with the info. Just...stay out of it now, okay? Don't go back to the clinic. Get out of town if you can and let me handle it."

"I didn't know who to call, but I hoped you didn't just disappear. That maybe you were braver than me and found someone who could help."

I hesitated for half a second. "You were right to call. The people I'm with know how to make this stop."

I ended the call and stared at the screen for a moment, my hand trembling around the phone. The weight of Marcy's words pressed down on my chest, thick and suffocating. My stomach twisted as my thoughts spiraled.

If I had looked harder or said something to Lainie sooner, they might not have had the opportunity to do another trial run...whatever that even was.

The bathroom door creaked open behind me, and Talon filled the doorway. His bare chest rose and fell as his gaze swept the room as though he was searching for a threat. His hair was still mussed from being asleep, but it didn't take away from the intensity of his focus, or his rugged sexiness.

"What happened?"

The concern in his rough voice hit me like a gut punch. I tried to speak, but the words got stuck in my throat.

He crossed the small room in two long strides, his hand coming up to brush against my cheek. "Tamara."

"I messed up," I whispered. "I should've seen it. I worked there and didn't know. People got hurt. Maybe even died. And I just...didn't see what was happening. And when I finally did, I ran."

His jaw flexed, and something dark flickered behind his eyes. His voice was low and fierce as he commanded, "Don't."

I blinked up at him.

"You don't carry this," he said, cupping the back of my neck and pulling me in until our foreheads touched. "I do."

My breath caught.

"You're mine. And if these bastards try to get to you, they'll have to kill me first."

Everything inside me cracked. The fear, the guilt, the shame. I didn't know how to hold it anymore. But somehow, I didn't feel like I had to, with his words anchoring me.

Talon didn't pull away. He stayed right there, forehead pressed to mine, one hand cradling the back of my neck while the other curled around my waist. He held me together just by being close.

"Marcy called. She's one of the nurses I worked with."

His muscles tensed, but he stayed right where he was. "What did she say?"

I explained about the trial run before whispering, "It's all too much."

"That's why I'm here," he rasped. "You don't need to carry this alone. You have me to do the heavy lifting on shit like this now, baby."

His lips brushed my forehead, and the dam inside me cracked again. Not in the same way as earlier. This wasn't fear. It was relief mixed with something deeper.

Sometimes, all you could do was cry it out. That was exactly what Talon gave me, holding me through my tears. When they passed, I lifted my face. His eyes met mine, dark and dangerous, but so full of caring that my chest ached.

"Better?"

"Yeah." I sniffled. "But only because of you."

He brushed the tears from my cheeks with the pads of his thumbs. "Good."

"Why do you make me feel so safe?"

His expression didn't change, but emotion flared in his gray-blue orbs. Then he leaned in and kissed me like he was staking his claim. There was no hesitation or slow build. His mouth crashed into mine, hot and demanding. I gasped, and he took full advantage, his tongue sweeping in and claiming every inch of me.

His fingers tightened at my waist as he lifted me to my feet before backing me against the wall.

This kiss made me feel like I was his entire world. As though this was the only way he knew how to tell me I wasn't alone anymore.

And oh boy, did I need it.

I kissed him back with everything I had, tangling my hands in his hair to pull him closer. My knees felt shaky, and my breath was unsteady, but I didn't care. Not when he poured so much into the press of his lips and swipe of his tongue against mine. When Talon finally pulled back, his chest rose and fell like he'd run a mile.

His thumb brushed over my cheek. "You're mine. Doesn't matter what comes next. You're not facing it alone."

I didn't trust myself to speak, so I just nodded and leaned into his chest.

He wrapped both arms around me and held me there for a long moment. Eventually, he nudged my chin with his knuckles, coaxing me to look up. "Come back to bed."

That sounded like exactly what I needed right now. "Okay."

He fired off a quick text about Marcy's call to one of his club brothers, and we climbed back under the covers. With his arms wrapped around me, Talon tilted my head back to kiss me again. It quickly grew heated and led to another round of sex.

After two more orgasms, sleep came easier than it had in days. And Talon never let go.

11

SAVAGE

After sleeping for a couple more hours, we got up, showered, dressed, and made our way to the kitchen for lunch. When we finished, I took my girl to the lounge, where we tended to hang out unless we were outside.

I had Tamara tucked against me on the leather couch, one arm slung low around her waist and the other draped across the back. She was curled in close, her cheek resting over my heart like it was her favorite spot. And hell if it wasn't mine too.

We relaxed together, lazy and content. Enjoying the kind of quiet that didn't happen often around the compound.

Although it was never completely silent around here. Across the room, Wrecker and Hawk were perched at the bar, arguing over which kind of bike oil gave a better burn-off smell. Ridiculous shit. But they were both dead serious about it, and the one-liners were flying. Hawk, sharp-tongued and dry as the desert, was poking Wrecker's last nerve. Wrecker, for his part, looked like he was one sentence away from launching a fucking barstool.

Tamara giggled softly against my chest.

Damn, that sound did something to me.

I looked down at her and got lost in the little smile tugging at her lips and the way she burrowed in like she never wanted to leave. My chest got tight, and I wondered how the hell I'd lived without this—without her—for so long.

The door to the kitchen swung open, and Rhiannon walked in with her and Viper's son on her hip. The kid was four months old, full of chubby limbs and bright eyes. He was squirming like he had someplace to be and no damn clue how to get there. I had to admit, even my grumpy ass couldn't help turning soft by all the cute kids running around.

Tamara perked up instantly. "Hi, Rhiannon! Oh my goodness, look at Harvey. I saw him a couple of days ago, and I feel like he's already getting bigger." She reached out eagerly. "Can I hold him?"

Rhiannon didn't hesitate, looking grateful as hell.

She handed over her son with a small sigh of relief and an affectionate eye roll. "Be my guest. I think my arms are going numb. He's teething. And I swear, the little wiggle-worm never stops moving."

Tamara pulled Harvey close, cooing at him as she bounced him gently on her lap while he flailed and babbled with pure baby nonsense. Watching her hold him—soft, playful, lit up from the inside—hit me straight in the chest, sending warmth to every part of me.

Fuck, she was gorgeous. I couldn't stop watching her. She looked so natural. So right. And I wanted it more than ever before. Her, just like that. Holding my kid. Ours.

Pictures of her in our future flashed through my mind, round and glowing, my ring on her hand and my baby growing inside her. And yeah, I'd be the one losing my shit every damn time she waddled too far from my reach or someone dared to look at her wrong.

I was seconds away from hauling her upstairs and working on that future again when Deviant walked in from the hallway that led to our offices. His expression was sharp, and his gaze met mine immediately. He jerked his chin toward the hallway, and I nodded.

I curled my fingers firmly around Tamara's jaw and turned her face up for a quick, hard kiss. "Be right back, baby."

She looked at Deviant curiously but didn't say a word.

Since there was no chance that I would ever let her go, we'd spent a little time earlier talking about how things worked within the club. I would never lie to her, but she'd have to accept that there would always be things I couldn't talk to her about. Times when I'd have to leave, and she wouldn't know why or where I was going. I couldn't discuss club business unless specifically given permission.

All this biotech shit revolved around her, so she'd been kept more in the loop. After chewing on it for a few minutes, she'd just said, "I can live with that."

If we hadn't been in the lounge, I'd have kissed the fuck outta her.

So when she didn't push for answers, just nodding to show that her trust was unshakable, I fell even harder. Pride mixed with satisfaction, and I silently cursed Deviant for cockblocking me.

Following him down the hall, I spotted Fox and Maverick already waiting near the prez's office. Deviant didn't waste time. "The message you sent me this morning about Tamara's friend Marcy? You were right to be worried."

I tensed. It wasn't like I hadn't guessed that, but I hated knowing how the confirmation would affect Tamara. "What did you find?"

"A fucking lot," he said grimly. "There's a building just over the line one town over. It looks abandoned, but recon showed that the inside's been retrofitted into a makeshift medical facility."

"How the fuck did this situation end up in our fucking backyard?" Fox growled.

Deviant looked hesitant, his eyes darting to me before going back to our prez.

My eyes narrowed. "What?"

"There's some evidence that they set up shop near here shortly after Tamara started working for them."

"Are you saying she's involved?" My tone was low and dangerous, a warning that he'd better consider his next words very carefully.

"Of course not." Deviant growled, then sighed. "Or not directly anyway."

I waited for an explanation.

"Dug a little deeper into the building they're using. The previous owner was Mike Hurst."

My brow shot up. "Tamara's dad?"

"I'm thinking they found out about the properties he was selling when they did the background
check before hiring her."

Silence descended, thick and heavy.

Then Deviant broke the quiet. "There's more."

Maverick expelled a harsh breath. "Movement?"

"All damn day," Deviant grunted. "People goin'
in but only employees coming back out. No doubt
they're moving in a group of new test subjects."

"Same company?" Maverick asked.

Deviant pressed his lips together, clearly reluctant to go on. "Same shell funding it, same routing
numbers, same lead tech. But the listed owner...it's
Tamara."

"What the fuck?" I shouted.

Before I could seriously lose my shit, Deviant
plowed on. "They copied her signature for the sale
straight from her employment application. She
never noticed the identity theft because it was paid
for with cash. Looks like they were setting her up to
take the fall for them if necessary. Probably why
things got weird the second she looked a little
deeper."

I was reeling from all this information and how
the hell to process it.

"Also, there's another mobile clinic on the edge

of town. This one is a smaller operation, out of a large van."

"Bastards are spreading like a fucking virus," Fox snarled. "This shit has gone far enough. We take it down tonight." Then his gaze locked with mine. "And when the last body clears that building..."

He didn't finish the sentence. He didn't have to.

I nodded once.

Finally.

I was gonna get to light a fucking match and watch their world go up in flames.

They moved to handle the rest of the planning, but my mind was already back on Tamara.

"Savage."

I glanced up to see Stone had joined us. "Make sure the destruction looks like it was done deliberately. Deviant and I will take care of the legal documents to ensure Tamara isn't connected, then I'll file an insurance claim for them. Being investigated for insurance fraud will be a great addition to the other charges they'll face."

"Fine," I agreed, glancing in the direction of the lounge.

Maverick clapped a hand on my shoulder and shoved. "Go. Only thing that's gonna keep you tame is your girl."

Yeah, tame wasn't anywhere near what I had in mind for Tamara.

I went back and found her still on the couch, Harvey now passed out in her arms while she whispered some lullaby I didn't recognize. I crouched in front of her and ran a hand up her thigh. "Come with me, baby."

She looked up at me, instantly alert. I took her hand and helped her up. I waited while she passed Harvey back to Rhiannon, then I led Tamara back to our room without another word.

Once we were inside, I closed the door and turned to face her.

"Headed out tonight," I said, my tone even. "Another raid. We know where they're keeping the people for the trial. It's local."

I kept my explanation simple and left all the other shit for another time.

Her breath caught. "You're going?"

"Yeah."

Her lip trembled before she could stop it. "I knew you would. It's the kind of stuff you guys do. But I'm scared." She tried for a sassy smile, but it wobbled. "I kind of like you. A lot. Probably all those amazing orgasms, but still, I don't want anything to happen to you."

"I fucking adore you, baby," I told her honestly as I stepped in close, brushing my knuckles down her cheek. "Nothing's gonna keep me from coming back to you. Not now. Not ever." One corner of my mouth lifted. "If my good girl wants to come, I'll—"

Tamara surged forward, wrapping her arms around my neck and pulling me in like she couldn't wait another second to taste me. The kiss started slowly. Soft lips, teasing breaths, the brush of her tongue against mine. It was everything. A promise. A fucking prayer.

But the second she moaned, quiet and needy, a switch flipped inside me. Just like that, I was done being gentle.

My hands fisted the hem of her shirt, pulling it up and off in one smooth move. Then I yanked her leggings and panties down and helped her kick them away.

"Fucking hell," I grunted before my lips were on hers again.

I didn't break the kiss or even let her breathe without me. I just backed her toward the wall, step by step, until her spine hit the hard surface with a soft thud. She gasped when my thigh shoved between hers, pressing up against her core, and I felt the heat of her slick through my jeans.

Her head tipped back, giving me better access. I licked up her neck before sinking my teeth into the soft skin just beneath her jaw. She shuddered, and my cock throbbed hard enough to hurt.

"You know what I'm about to do, don't you?" I growled against the flushed skin of her throat. "Gonna fuck my baby so deep you won't remember what empty feels like."

"Talon," she whimpered, her voice catching on my name. "Please."

"That's right," I rasped, sliding a hand between her thighs. "Beg me to fill you."

My middle finger glided through her slick folds, and I groaned, "You're soaked already. You want it, don't you?"

"Yes," she breathed, hips rocking forward, chasing the pleasure my hand could give her.

I grabbed her thighs and lifted her like she weighed nothing, wrapping her legs tight around my waist. Her breath caught as I pinned her to the wall, my body caging hers completely.

"Not just sex tonight," I growled, my voice low and rough as gravel. "This is mating, Tamara. You're mine, and I'm gonna brand you in every way. Starting with a swollen belly so everyone who looks at you knows you're mine."

She whimpered my name again, a desperate sound that cracked something wide open in me, making my hunger for her nearly unbearable.

"Gonna fuck you so full of come, your body won't know how to be anything except mine. You want that, baby?"

"Yes," she breathed. "Oh yes."

Her hands pulled at my cut, so I used my hips to hold her up while I ripped it off and tossed it to the floor, my shirt quickly joining it.

"Take me out, baby," I ordered.

She made quick work of my belt, then unzipped my pants before wrapping her hot little hand as far as it could go around my shaft.

"Fuck, yes," I groaned.

She took me out, squeezed once, then used her thumb to flick my piercing.

"Oh, shit!" I yelled, my pelvis thrusting into her palm.

I was gone. There was nothing left of me but the need to fuck. Hard. Fast. Deep. To make my woman scream while I filled her womb with my seed.

I slammed inside her, burying myself to the hilt. Her head fell back against the wall, and her nails raked down my shoulders, her entire body trembling around me. Tight. Hot. Perfect. Her pussy squeezed me like it already knew I was the only one who'd ever be inside her. Knew who owned it.

"Mine," I grunted. "My pussy. Say it."

"Yours!" she cried out, her inner muscles pulsing around my cock.

I fucked her like I was branding her from the inside out, my hips slamming into hers with punishing force, one arm locked under her thigh, the other cupping the back of her skull to protect her from getting hurt again. My lips never stopped— kissing her mouth, neck, and jaw, while whispering every filthy, possessive thought that filled my mind.

It wasn't soft. It wasn't sweet.

It was feral.

"Tight little pussy was made for me," I growled, my forehead pressed to hers. "Made for taking my cock and having my babies. You hear me?"

"Yes! Yes! Talon!"

I pounded in and out, stretching her, taking her, owning her. "Fuck! Oh fuck, Tamara! That's it, baby! Fuck!"

Her walls clamped down around me, tight and greedy, and I felt her climax slam into her like a freight train. Her body bowed, her mouth open on a silent cry, her nails sinking deep into my back.

I followed a heartbeat later, thrusting so deep I

could've sworn our souls tangled. My piercing bumped against her cervix as I shot load after load until I'd emptied every drop inside her.

I held her there, pressed to the wall, both of us panting like we'd just survived a raging storm. Then again, that wasn't all that far off. When Tamara and I collided, it was as if the world was thrown into chaos. My heart thundered, her breaths were ragged, and for a long moment, we didn't say anything. We didn't need to.

Eventually, when my legs were steady enough, I carried her to the bed and gently set her down. Settling myself on top of her, I kissed her again, slow and reverent, my lips moving over hers like a vow.

Because even when I was at my most primal—especially then—she was still everything.

12

SAVAGE

I left her sleeping. Naked, sated, and wrapped in the sheets like a gift I didn't deserve.

The room smelled like her. Sex, sweat, and mine. Her pale skin was flushed, lips kiss-swollen, wild curls tangled on my pillow like spun honey. It took everything I had to tear myself from that bed. To walk out knowing if she woke up alone, she'd worry over me.

But this bullshit needed to fucking end.

No matter what happened tonight, I was ready to move forward with my future.

With Tamara.

I was done holding back from my woman. When I got home, I'd give her my property patch and slide my ring on her finger.

Sav

e clubhouse was quiet and dark as I stalked through it, my boots echoing against the concrete as I stepped into the garage and found everyone already waiting.

Fox leaned against the hood of his blacked-out Charger, arms crossed, glaring at Racer, who sat behind the wheel with a giant grin.

"Not happening, citizen," Fox barked. "Get in one of the fucking SUVs before I break your nose on the steering wheel. And if you get so much as a drop of blood anywhere, you'll be swallowing your teeth next."

Wrecker was perched on the edge of the work-bench, flipping a wrench between his fingers. Whiskey leaned back against the wall, checking the magazines in the guns lined up on the table next to him. We all had our own firearms, but the club had a cache of weapons for when we needed something untraceable or specialized. As our sergeant at arms, he was our chief security officer, so among his many duties, he oversaw the club-owned armory.

Hawk crouched near the front tire of his bike, checking the pressure and talking casually with Maverick and Hunter like we weren't heading into a war zone.

"'Bout time," Wrecker muttered when he spotted

me. "We figured your girl wrapped herself around you so tight you couldn't pry her off."

"Couldn't or wouldn't?" Whiskey added with a smirk.

"Didn't ask for commentary, assholes," I growled, grabbing my helmet.

Fox pushed off the Charger and met my gaze. "Got the layout?"

I nodded once. "Seven rooms. One of 'em used for housing the patients. Two for procedures. There's also a lab and an office. The last ones look like storage. And they're using the alley behind the building as a patient drop."

"The test subjects?" Fox asked.

"Six of them inside. All sedated. Four women, two men. No IDs. No clothes. Just medical bracelets and tracking chips."

Fox's jaw ticked. "We take them first." He shot a look at Racer. "Get the fuck outta my car, go grab the bag of clothes Dahlia left inside by the door, then get your ass in the SUV and meet us there."

Racer's grin was gone, all business now. "On it," he muttered, climbing out of the Charger and stalking back into the clubhouse.

"Secure the evidence next," Fox continued. "Then we get the bastards."

Maverick tossed me a small duffel. "Zip ties, hoods, and a couple of extras in case you get bored."

Wrecker snorted. "He doesn't get bored. He gets bloodthirsty."

I gave him a look. "Keep talkin'. You'll see which one I am tonight."

The tension crackled as we mounted up, engines snarling to life. The ride out was a blur of cold wind, the growl of our hogs loud in the dark night.

It didn't take long to reach our destination. Just a few backroads and a grim silence stretched between the thunder of engines.

We parked the bikes four blocks out—close enough to move fast but far enough to avoid attention. The old canning plant behind us was nothing but broken windows and rusted metal, forgotten by everyone but stray cats and weeds. Fine by me. I was in no mood for witnesses.

Midnight met us at the corner of the property. "Techs just left for a dinner break. Got about twenty minutes till they're back. I'll be in the van across the street monitoring the perimeter."

He handed Hawk an earpiece since he was the only one on comms tonight. It left the rest of us with no distractions so we wouldn't let down our guard and get caught unaware.

We slipped to the building like shadows. The security here was a step up from the storage facility, but Deviant was already in the system. As I approached the back door, there was a beep, then the red flashing light on the lock turned green. Still, I waited.

"All clear," Hawk murmured a few seconds later. "Cameras inside are looped. Only Deviant can see the feeds."

The door creaked when it opened. Even knowing the employees were gone, I hesitated, making sure we weren't surprised by a fourth tech we'd somehow missed.

No one appeared, and I didn't hear another sound, so I wedged the door to stay open and stepped inside.

The smell hit first. Stale air that hadn't moved in hours. Bleach. The sharp scent of chemicals. But none of that completely masked the smell of human sickness.

Hawk and I took point while Whiskey and Maverick swept left. Fox and Hunter circled right, with Wrecker covering our backs.

It didn't take long to find them.

We cleared nearly every room when we heard a soft moan. Then another.

The sound led us down a dim hall until we reached a locked door. Again, I waited until the red light turned green, then pushed inward. The moment the door swung open, I felt like I'd been punched in the gut.

"Son of a bitch!"

I stalked in, chest rising with every breath like I couldn't get enough air. My fists clenched at my sides.

This room was colder than the rest. Glancing around, I saw no uniforms, no proper equipment—just makeshift crap that screamed rushed setup and no accountability.

Tamara's words echoed in my head. Those names that had vanished, the files that didn't match up. This was where they went.

The patients—*victims*, I silently amended—lay on narrow folding beds that lined against the walls. Four women and two men who were barely covered by a thin sheet. IVs dangled from rolling poles. Machines beeped in soft, erratic rhythms.

"Status?" Fox asked from behind me.

"Alive," I growled. "Barely. Drugged. But breathing."

"They restrained?" Wrecker asked, stepping into the room beside me.

"Some of them." I nodded toward a young man on the corner bed nearest us. Early twenties, wrists strapped, and bruises across his jaw. "This one fought back."

Wrecker's lip curled. "Bet they didn't like that."

Hawk's eyes glittered with restrained fury as he took in the scene. "They aren't trying to kill them. They want to fucking use them. To test, to control. It's a game to these sick bastards."

"Get Blade on the line," Fox snapped as his eyes swept the room.

"Already here," Blade's voice called out as he entered through the rear with two brothers pushing stretchers from a club-owned ambulance. "Mav told me about the run. Figured we'd need a medevac."

Two younger paramedics followed them. Trusted kids who knew how to keep their mouths shut.

"Start loading them. Quietly," Fox ordered.

We moved fast—removing IVs, helping the groggy patients to sit up, and dressing them in clean sweatpants and shirts from the emergency duffels. Then Blade and his team got to work checking vitals and transferring bodies to stretchers. They'd only brought in four, so I carried the other two out to the rig myself, one cradled in each arm like broken things

I was sworn to protect. Once they were carefully secured, the two paramedics climbed into the back with the patients. Blade shut the double doors, and the lock clicked from the inside.

"You good?" Fox asked him.

Blade gave a single nod as he stalked to the front and yanked open the driver's side door. "I'll get them to the hospital. Already called ahead. They've cleared an intake room."

The Iron Rogues owned just about every inch of Old Bridge. Not just land and businesses but also the police, politicians, and we'd practically built the hospital. Blade had a clinic on the compound, but he also worked shifts in the ER. Partly because he wanted to, but it also made it easier for him to be listed as the physician on record whenever the club used the facility for injuries that needed more care but kept quiet.

"Keep me posted," Fox said.

Blade jerked his chin up before hopping into the front cab. The low rumble of the ambulance engine was the only sound as he pulled onto the road.

Back inside the facility, we collected vials and specimens, as well as some paperwork and other evidence that would only be stored here, rather than the warehouse.

"Find much?" Hunter asked, popping his head into the lab where Hawk and I collected information.

"Too fucking much," I muttered, tossing another file into a half-full body bag. "These assholes logged everything. Medications. Dosages. Reactions. They didn't even bother to try to disguise that these are medical trials."

"Cocky," Hawk sneered.

"Fucking stupid."

Wrecker and Mav were taking out the last load when we heard the front door open down the hall. It scraped over the linoleum, then there were voices. Three sets of footsteps. Laughter.

The techs were back.

Fox appeared beside me like a ghost. "Take them."

We waited until they turned the corner before pouncing. One lead scientist in a white coat, clipboard still in hand. Two younger assistants behind him, wide-eyed and twitchy.

They didn't even get a scream out before we were on 'em. They put up a feeble struggle, but they weren't fighters. Not even close. I zip-tied wrists, put hoods on their heads, and *accidentally* shoved one into the wall hard enough to make him whimper. No blood, though. Not yet. Just enough fear to make them shut up and cooperate.

Racer pulled up in one of the club's black SUVs with the side door already open. "Got room for three jackasses. Let's go."

Fox pointed at the back seats. "Take them to The Room. And don't drive like the reckless son of a bitch you are on the track. Stone needs them breathing to question them."

I stalked forward, jaw clenched, every inch of me coiled in rage. "Stone can have them after—"

Fox's gaze cut to mine. "Stone first."

I didn't reply. I just stared at him. Deadpan.

He took a step closer. "We need them to talk. To name names. You break them before Stone gets what he needs, and you screw the whole case. You gonna convince me they'll be capable of that after you're done with them?"

I gritted my teeth. "Can't promise anything."

"Exactly. You know I'm right, Savage."

My fists curled at my sides as I snarled, "Someone needs to bleed."

"They will," he replied quietly. "But not until we get what we need."

I sucked in several breaths, my nostrils flaring

and my jaw clenched. Eventually, I was in enough control to nod in agreement.

Maverick walked over and shoved a red gas can into my chest. Then he held up a matchbook tucked between two fingers.

"Fire's cleaner than fists," he said, voice dry. "Burn it down."

"Leave evidence, not bodies," Hunter reminded me.

My hands clenched around the red gas can like it was an extension of my rage. Then I snatched the matchbook and looked at the building around me.

All this had been used to hurt people. To end lives. To drag my woman into something she never asked for.

I turned the container over and set it on the nearest shelf, watching the liquid drain until a puddle was on the floor.

My shoulders were tight with fury, and I exhaled hard.

Then I lit a match.

13

TAMARA

I couldn't sleep. The bed was far too empty without Talon. Even wearing one of his shirts and clutching his hoodie didn't help. I kept staring at the door as though he might walk through it at any second. But he didn't.

Every minute that passed without Talon made me wonder what was happening. If he was okay.

Eventually, I gave up trying and slid out of bed. After tugging on a pair of sweatpants and comfy socks, I padded down the hall. The big lounge area was softly lit with a couple of old lamps and had a low murmur of voices coming from the TV. I wasn't surprised to find a few of the old ladies curled up on the black leather couches with knit blankets and half-finished mugs of hot drinks.

Sadie looked up from her seat, her slightly rounded belly pronounced under a big black T-shirt that her husband Hunter had probably given her. "Trouble sleeping?"

I nodded, hugging myself tightly. "The waiting is so hard."

Dahlia was sitting next to Sadie and patted the cushion beside her. "Come sit. It's easier when you have company. Molly has the twins, so I can wait here for Kye. We take turns during club business."

I sank down next to her and let the warmth of the room settle into my bones. Sheila sat across from us in an armchair, her knitting needles clicking steadily. She glanced over at me with a motherly smile. "You want tea? Or some hot cocoa? I made some in case I found you girls waiting here on your men."

I shook my head and whispered, "Thanks, but I'm okay."

"You look like you're gonna vibrate out of your skin," Sadie murmured gently. "You love him already, don't you?"

I blinked fast, the sting behind my eyes catching me off guard. "I think I did the moment I saw him. I just didn't admit it until now."

"You're not alone in that," Sheila reassured me

with a soft smile. "Savage proved to be just like his club brothers when he met you. When an Iron Rogue finds their one, they choose them with everything they've got."

"I wish I'd been brave enough to tell him how I felt before they left," I admitted. "What if something goes wrong?"

"Then he'll crawl back bloody just to hold you," Dahlia replied without hesitation. "Just like Kye would do for me."

The room quieted after that. Eventually, someone draped a blanket over my legs and dimmed the lights.

I curled up on the end of the couch, hugging Talon's hoodie to my chest and breathing in his scent. Only then did the knot in my stomach loosen enough for sleep to finally find me.

I wasn't sure how much time had passed when a hand brushed against my cheek. I jolted awake, heart leaping before I was even fully conscious.

"Easy, baby," a rough voice murmured. "It's just me."

Talon was back.

I blinked, trying to shake off the fog of sleep, but the second I saw his face, the knot in my chest unraveled so fast that I almost couldn't breathe. He crouched beside the couch, his palm cradling my cheek and his eyes locked on mine like I was the only thing in the world that mattered.

"You're okay," I whispered, reaching for him with shaking fingers.

"I told you I would be." His voice was low and tired as his thumb swept under my eye, catching the moisture I hadn't realized was there. "Didn't I promise to come back to you?"

I nodded before throwing my arms around his neck and burying my face against his shoulder. He was warm, solid...and everything I needed.

Talon stood in one smooth motion, lifting me into his arms as though I weighed nothing. I didn't care that we were in the middle of the lounge with people around us. It didn't matter to me if anyone saw us as I curled into him and held on.

He carried me down the hallway and back to our room without saying a word. The door clicked shut behind us, and then I was in his lap on the bed, strad-dling him, my knees on either side of his hips. I cupped his face in my hands and took in every inch of him.

"You scared the hell out of me," I breathed.

"I hated leaving you," he rasped. "But it was necessary."

I leaned in, brushing my lips across his. When I started to pull back, he tangled his fist in the back of my hair to hold me close as he deepened the kiss.

I was breathless when he finally let me go, but I still managed to whisper, "I love you." The words tumbled out in a rush before I could second-guess them, but I had no regrets about saying them. "I didn't say it before, and I should've. I don't care if it's too soon because I love you so much."

His eyes darkened, and a deep growl rumbled up his chest before he devoured me like a man coming undone. His kiss told me he felt the same, but when he finally ripped his mouth from mine, he gave me the words too.

"You better," he growled. "I love you so fucking much, Tamara. Never lettin' you go."

Talon shifted us slightly on the bed. One arm remained wrapped around my waist as he reached toward the nightstand and pulled open the bottom drawer. When he turned back to face me, he held something in his hand.

My breath caught the moment I realized what it was. My name was right there, stitched on the front of the black leather vest. And on the back, in stark, unapologetic letters: PROPERTY OF SAVAGE.

"Oh my goodness," I breathed.

He held the vest out to me. "Fox gave this to me yesterday. But I didn't want all the shit with the clinic overshadowing makin' you my old lady."

"Talon," I whispered, my fingers trembling as I reached out to touch it.

"You already wear my shirt, sleep in my bed, and hold every damn part of me. Everyone already knows you belong to me." His voice was thick with emotion in a way I hadn't heard before. "But I wanted to make it official."

I swallowed hard. "Even without the property patch, I was absolutely yours."

"Still need you to wear it," he murmured. "Because you're mine, and I want the world to know it."

I blinked fast, my chest aching with how much I felt for him. "This means I'm your old lady now?"

His grin was slow and dark. "No, baby. That happened the second you let me touch you like you were already mine."

I laughed through the tears threatening to spill. "Okay, but now it's stitched in thread, too. So nobody can miss it."

"Damn right, it is." His expression shifted, eyes turning fierce again as he pulled me against his chest.

"You're mine, Tamara. That doesn't change. Not ever."

Talon leaned in and pressed a kiss to my temple, followed by my cheek, then the corner of my mouth. They were soft touches that made my breath hitch. But when I turned my head and brushed my lips against his, the tenderness between us snapped into something else entirely.

He growled low in his throat and flipped me onto my back, pinning me with the weight of his body. "You're mine."

"I know," I whispered, heart pounding. "And you're mine too."

"Damn fucking straight." He kissed me hard and deep. It was a claiming, his tongue sweeping into my mouth while his hand slid beneath the hem of my shirt to splay over my bare stomach. He pulled back just enough to look down at me, his thumb tracing lazy circles against my skin.

"I'm gonna put a kid in you," he murmured, his voice rough. "Might be tonight if I haven't already done it. Soon, you'll be full of me, wearing my ring, my patch. Every fucking thing I can give you. All of me."

My breath caught, and I didn't even try to stop the rush of emotion that flooded me. Talon didn't make promises he didn't intend to keep, so I knew I could count on the future he described.

"Your ring?"

He brushed his thumb over my finger. "Already ordered it, just waitin' on the jeweler since I wanted the sapphire to be a perfect match for your eyes."

I loved that he had put so much thought into my engagement ring. There were details to figure out, like me leaving Lainie without a roommate, but I had no doubt that we'd work it all out. Together.

"I want all of it," I whispered, not trying to hide everything I felt now that we both knew where we stood with each other. "You and me. Babies. Building a family."

His eyes burned hotter. "You'll have it."

He kissed me again, slower this time. Like he had all the time in the world to remind me who I belonged to...because he did.

EPILOGUE
SAVAGE

The Midnight Rebel smelled like wood polish, whiskey, and the faintest trace of lemon cleaner. It was quiet for now, with just the hum of the old jukebox in standby mode and the thudding of my boots against the scuffed floorboards as I restocked the liquor shelves, checked the register, refilled the garnish containers, and got the bar ready to open. It was Friday night, and we had a full house expected later. Everything needed to be ready, or the place would descend into pure chaos. Especially when I'd taken the night off.

I moved on autopilot since my mind wasn't really in the bar. It was with Tamara, tucked away in my office, nose-deep in one of her textbooks, probably chewing on the edge of her pen while she tried to memorize a list of Latin terms or some shit like that. And our six-month old daughter. Calida already had me wrapped tighter than my fists in a street fight. I'd take the world apart with my bare hands for my baby girl, no questions asked.

The front door opened, and Hawk stomped inside, muttering to himself.

"Late," I grunted when he finally noticed I was in the room.

"Take it up with Midnight," he snapped as he marched over to the bar. "New assignment."

He snatched a glass and a bottle of his favorite whiskey. After pouring two fingers, he drank it all in one swallow.

I waited, knowing he'd keep ranting if I let him, and I could get a better idea of why he looked like he was on the edge of his sanity.

"Fucking client briefing." He scowled as he poured another glass and tossed the entire contents down his throat again. "What kind of a name is Gemma, anyway?"

He pivoted on his heel and disappeared into the kitchen.

Gemma.

My lips curved into a smirk. From the way he'd

been riled up, I should've figured this was about a woman. *His* woman.

Chuckling, I finished with the last of the prep and wiped my palms on a bar towel, before heading to my office. Hawk was forgotten, and my heart kicked up with every step.

I pushed the door open quietly, and there they were. My reasons for existing.

Tamara was curled in my chair with her legs tucked under her. She was wearing one of my T-shirts knotted at the waist and a pair of soft black leggings. Her hair was twisted up in a messy knot, a pencil stabbed through it, making me think of a naughty librarian. Her laptop was open, her textbook sprawled across her lap, a highlighter gripped between two fingers as she read with a furrowed brow.

Hmmm. Naughty student was probably a better comparison.

Beside her, our daughter swung slowly back and forth in her baby swing, soft gurgles escaping her chubby little mouth. She was dressed in a pink onesie with ruffles at the shoulders and the words "I'm proud my mommy can't resist her biker" on the front, and tiny socks that never stayed on. Her pacifier was in her mouth, but she kept trying to spit it out.

Her bright cornflower-blue eyes flicked toward me and widened like she *knew* who I was. Knew I was *hers*. She squealed, a sound that hit me dead in the center of the chest, and my heart squeezed.

Tamara looked up and smiled. A sweet, happy one that wrecked me every time.

"Hey," she said softly, eyes still a little glassy from staring at her notes. "All set?"

"Yeah," I murmured, stepping inside and shutting the door behind me. "Bar's ready. Staff's prepped. I'm done for the night."

Her round lips curved up. "You have the night off?"

"Yep."

"Whatever will we do with ourselves?" she asked, batting her eyelashes. It was amazing how she could make me laugh and as hard as a fucking rock at the same time.

"Got some ideas," I told her with a wink.

Giggling, she turned in the chair slightly, stretching her arms overhead. I let my gaze drag over her. The curve of her waist, the soft swell of her tits, the way her belly had never quite gone back to the way it used to be. I didn't want it to. Every mark, every line she'd earned from carrying our girl made her a fucking warrior. She was sexy as hell. And all mine.

"You almost done?" I asked, nodding at the book.

She groaned. "I have to finish reviewing this clinical ethics chapter, then quiz myself on pharmacology." She rolled her eyes and slumped dramatically. "It never ends."

I stepped behind her, bent low, and pressed a kiss to the side of her neck, then dug my thumbs into her stiff muscles, ignoring the way her delighted moan felt like a fist wrapped around my shaft.

"That's 'cause you're doing something that matters." My voice was rough and quiet. "Told you I'd back you all the way. You're more than halfway done. That's more than most would've tried."

She leaned into me slightly, that familiar tension in her shoulders melting away. "Because of you," she whispered.

"*For* you," I corrected. "Always."

After the clinic fallout hit the news, the whole operation collapsed overnight. Corporate heads rolled, labs shut down, assets frozen. I'd made sure the worst of them never got back up again. Once the dust settled, I pushed her—gently but without giving her room to back out—to chase her original dream. A real nursing degree. A future on her terms. And she'd taken to it with the same quiet strength I saw in her the night I first carried her to safety. She amazed me every damn day.

I kissed the top of her head, then nodded toward the door. "Time to go home."

We quickly packed up her backpack, purse, and the diaper bag while Calida yawned like this was all beneath her. Then she promptly passed out the second her head hit the soft padding of her car seat.

The drive was less than fifteen minutes, but it felt longer. My heart beat hard the whole way, my palms damp as I hoped for the right reaction to my surprise.

Her fingers drummed absently on the console while she looked out the window, unaware of what was coming.

Finally, I pulled into the driveway and turned off the engine.

Tamara blinked, confused as she stared at the house in front of us. "Whose place is this?"

"Yours," I said simply. "Ours."

She turned to me, wide-eyed, mouth falling open slightly as she stared. The stone and wood structure was two stories, with a wraparound porch and warm light spilling from the inside like it had been waiting for her. For us.

I exited the car and jogged around to her side, opening her door and helping her to her feet.

"I...I don't understand," she whispered.

"It's home."

She stared at me with an awed expression as I unclipped Calida's seat and lifted it out. Holding the carrier on one arm, I grabbed Tamara's hand and pulled her toward the front door.

Inside, her steps slowed as she took it all in. The hardwood floors, wide open kitchen with the hanging pots and the island bar, and brick fireplace with the hearth already stacked. The oversized sofa, with a plush blanket tossed over the back.

Everything had been handpicked for comfort and warmth. For a family.

"You did this?" she gasped.

I chuckled. "Promised I'd never lie to you, baby, so I gotta be honest. The other old ladies had a big hand in picking all this shit out."

Tamara giggled and went up on her tiptoes to brush a kiss over my cheek. "I love you."

"Love you, too, baby." I leaned in for another kiss, but she danced away to explore the place.

When she stepped into the hallway and noticed

the number of doors lining it, she raised a brow, eyeing me suspiciously. "This is awfully big for just the three of us."

I smirked. "Don't worry, baby. We're gonna fill it."

She turned, one hand on her hip and an adorably sassy expression on her face. "Oh really? Just how many kids are you expecting me to pop out, exactly?"

I stepped closer, brushed a strand of hair behind her ear, and kissed the corner of her mouth. "However many you'll give me."

Tamara's breath hitched, and she looked at me with that expression that always made me feel like the luckiest man alive.

Taking her hand once more, I led her to the nursery and pushed the door open.

Her gasp was everything.

Because this one was all me. I hadn't let anyone step foot in this room. It had to be fucking perfect for my girls.

The room was warm, painted in soft sage and cream, bathed in the sunlight slanting through gauzy curtains. The crib, dresser, and rocking chair were all in honey-colored wood. Stuffed animals lined the shelves, and the bedding set was the exact one she'd pinned three separate times without realizing. I had

Deviant print out her old boards and spent weeks getting every detail right.

"You did this?" she asked, voice thick.

I nodded, then frowned when her eyes got suspiciously wet. I hated when she cried—even happy tears.

With a knowing smirk, she wiped away the moisture, then walked slowly into the room. She trailed her fingertips over the dresser and the top of the rocking chair, then bent over the crib to adjust a stuffed bunny.

I brought the baby carrier over and carefully set it inside the crib.

Tamara ran a fingertip over our daughter's soft cheek, then bent to kiss her forehead. Calida let out a soft sigh in her sleep, and my heart was so full it fucking ached as I watched them both.

After a minute, I stepped behind Tamara, gripped her hand, and pulled her gently toward the door.

"Come on," I rasped, picking up the baby monitor as we stepped out of the room, then quietly shutting the door.

Tamara let me lead her down the hall, past the other doors, to the primary bedroom. I opened it and guided her inside. This was the one other room I'd done alone. It was our space, and I hadn't wanted to share it with anyone, not even to let them help me pick out the paint color for the walls.

She walked to the center and did a complete turn, taking it all in. Low lighting, dark wood furniture, and a massive bed already turned down.

"It's beautiful. Perfect." Then she turned to me, eyes dark and knowing. "I take it we're not unpacking?"

I growled low in my throat, already backing her toward the bed. "Later."

My mouth caught hers in a kiss that promised everything.

Because tonight, I was going to worship her all over again.

And tomorrow, we'd start filling another room.

EPILOGUE
TAMARA

The late afternoon sun slanted through the windows of the Old Bridge free clinic's staff lounge, casting a gleam against the bulletin board I'd helped decorate earlier that week. The task had fallen to me because I was the only mom on the nursing staff. It was not exactly fair, but I didn't complain since I was happy to have a flexible position that allowed me to use the degree that had taken me so long to get while still having time for my husband and our children.

After what I'd seen at the mobile clinic, on top of what had happened to my mom, I wanted to help for real. Talon had encouraged me to go to nursing school, and I never would've made it through without him.

Juggling a growing family and my studies hadn't been easy, but I'd been luckier than most students because I had such a great support system between him and the Iron Rogues crew. If it weren't for Blade, the club's doctor, I wouldn't even have this job as a part-time float nurse since I'd only gone back to school long enough to become an LPN.

"Don't forget to clock out, Tamara," one of my coworkers called as she walked past.

"Got it," I smiled. "Thanks, Marie."

I finished entering a note into the charting system, then logged out and tucked my badge into my tote. My shift had ended a little early today, and I was excited to get home.

I stepped out into the fall breeze and zipped my jacket. Old Bridge was finally getting chilly, and I couldn't wait to get home and curl up under one of the soft throws I'd left on the couch.

Talon's bike rumbled to life from a spot on the far end of the parking lot before the door even shut all the way behind me. I grinned as he rolled to a stop, that familiar scowl tugging at his lips even though I knew he'd been watching for me since I texted that I was off early.

"You could've just come to pick me up on time

instead of stalking me from the lot," I teased as I walked over.

"Had to make sure no one else got any ideas," he muttered, pulling off his helmet and setting it aside. "You're too damn tempting."

I laughed, walking right into his open arms. "And you're ridiculous."

"That's not the insult you think it is, baby." He grinned at me. "'Cause it makes you the woman who married ridiculous."

"And I'd do it again," I whispered against his cut.

His arms tightened around me, and for a second, we just stood there. The world faded away like it always did when he held me like this.

"Come on," he finally said. "I promised Calida you'd be home before bedtime, and she's got that glare of yours when she's mad."

"She gets it from you," I muttered.

"Nope," he disagreed as he grabbed my helmet. "I've seen you mad. She's got your stubborn chin, too."

Our daughter was three going on thirty, and I adored every bossy inch of her. She was currently in a tutu phase and wanted to wear one with everything. She had also just discovered glitter glue, much to Talon's horror. But he never said no when she held her arms up because she had him wrapped around her finger tighter than any MC patch.

He helped me onto the bike, and I settled against his back with my arms around his waist. The ride home was quick, and I spotted the porch lights glowing as we pulled up to our house. The place still took my breath away sometimes. Every room had signs of our life together. Toys. Boots by the door. A framed photo of Calida covered in frosting from her last birthday. The pregnancy test under the cabinet that I planned to take tomorrow morning...after I told Talon what I suspected.

The second we walked in, I heard running footsteps. "Mama!"

Calida barreled into me, and I scooped her up, covering her cheeks in kisses. "Hey, cupcake! Did you miss me?"

"Yes," she whispered dramatically, clinging to me as though I'd been gone for days instead of barely seven hours.

"Missed you, too," I murmured as I set her back on her feet. "Were you good for Sheila while Daddy picked me up from work?"

"Uh-huh." She lifted her hand with her fingers splayed and whispered, "I gots tree cookies!"

"I thought that was our little secret," Sheila

chided as she padded into the living room behind our little whirlwind.

Calida giggled. "Oops, sorry."

Sheila ruffled her hair. "That's okay, sweetie."

"Cookies, huh?" I asked as I cuddled against Talon's side.

"Don't worry, there's some left for you two."

I patted my belly. "Lucky me."

"Troy got fussy, so I put him down, and he drifted right off for a nap," she explained as she handed Talon the baby monitor.

He gave her a chin lift. "Thanks."

There was a rumble of a bike in the driveway as Sheila shrugged on her jacket. "That'll be Tank, come to pick me up."

"Thanks so much for keeping an eye on her for us." I gave her a quick hug. "And the cookies."

"Any time." She beamed a smile at us before walking out the door.

Talon slung our daughter onto his shoulder like a sack of potatoes, making her shriek with laughter. "Show me where the cookies are, my little menace. Your mama needs a treat after working so hard."

I kicked off my shoes and followed them into the kitchen, sidling up to Talon after he set Calida on her feet again. "A cookie sounds great, but I can think of an even better treat."

He captured my mouth in a deep kiss before growling, "And you'll get that too, after we put her down for bed."

I ended up getting more than I bargained for. The pregnancy test I took the next day was negative, but the one a month later was positive. And it was twins.

Find out what happens with Hawk and Gemma!

And if you join our newsletter, you'll get a FREE copy of The Virgin's Guardian, which was banned on Amazon.

ABOUT THE AUTHOR

The writing duo of Elle Christensen and Rochelle Paige team up under the Fiona Davenport pen name to bring you sexy, insta-love stories filled with alpha males. If you want a quick & dirty read with a guaranteed happily ever after, then give Fiona Davenport a try!

Printed in Great Britain
by Amazon

63055400R00090